W9-AVQ-460

017
2018

AVON FREE PUBLIC LIBRARY

CURSE OF THE RED SCORPION

LIBRARIAN REVIEWER

Laurie K. Holland

Media Specialist (National Board Certified), Edina, MN

MA in Elementary Education, Minnesota State University, Mankato, MN

READING CONSULTANT

Elizabeth Stedem

Educator/Consultant, Colorado Springs, CO

MA in Elementary Education, University of Denver, CO

Graphic Sparks are published by Stone Arch Books,
151 Good Counsel Drive, P.O. Box 669,
Mankato, Minnesota 56002.
www.stonearchbooks.com

Copyright © 2006 by Stone Arch Books.

All rights reserved. No part of this publication may be reproduced
in whole or in part, or stored in a retrieval system, or transmitted in any
form or by any means, electronic, mechanical, photocopying, recording,
or otherwise, without written permission of the publisher.

Library of Congress Cataloging-in-Publication Data
Nickel, Scott.
    Curse of the Red Scorpion / by Scott Nickel; illustrated by Steve Harpster.
    p. cm. — (Graphic Sparks)
    ISBN-13: 978-1-59889-034-1 (hardcover)
    ISBN-10: 1-59889-034-4 (hardcover)
    1. Graphic novels. I. Harpster, Steve. II. Title. III. Series.
PN6727.N544C87 2006
741.5—dc22   2005026684

Summary: Mitchell was bored at the museum — until he saw the amazing Red Scorpion
of Manzitopia! Now he thinks the creature has followed him home. Do claws click in the
night? Does a stinger hide in the curtains? Will Mitchell trap the beast before he becomes
its next victim?

Art Director: Heather Kindseth
Production Manager: Sharon Reid
Production/Design: James Liebman, Mie Tsuchida
Production Assistance: Bob Horvath, Eric Murray

1 2 3 4 5 6 11 10 09 08 07 06

Printed in the United States of America.

CURSE OF THE RED SCORPION

BY SCOTT NICKEL

ILLUSTRATED BY STEVE HARPSTER

▼▼ STONE ARCH BOOKS
Minneapolis San Diego

J
GRAPHIC
NIC

c.1

CAST OF CHARACTERS

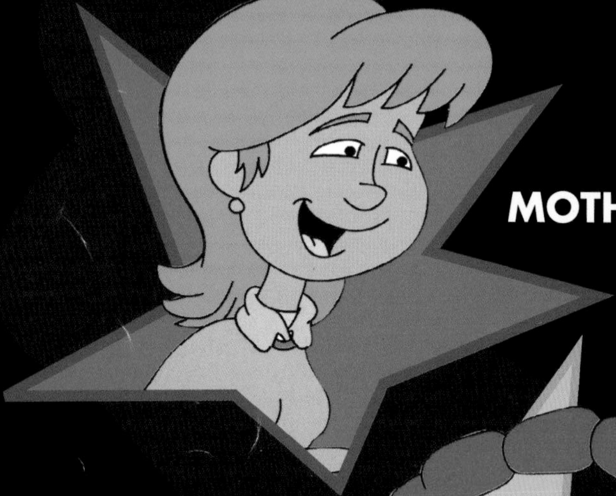

MOTHER

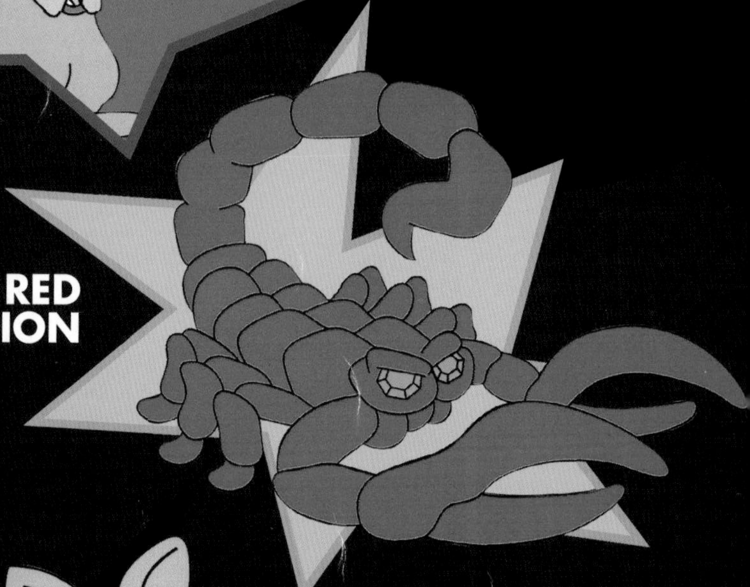

RED SCORPION

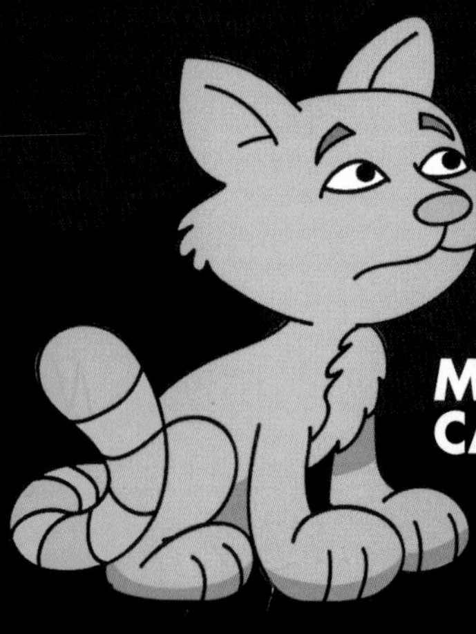

MITCHELL'S CAT

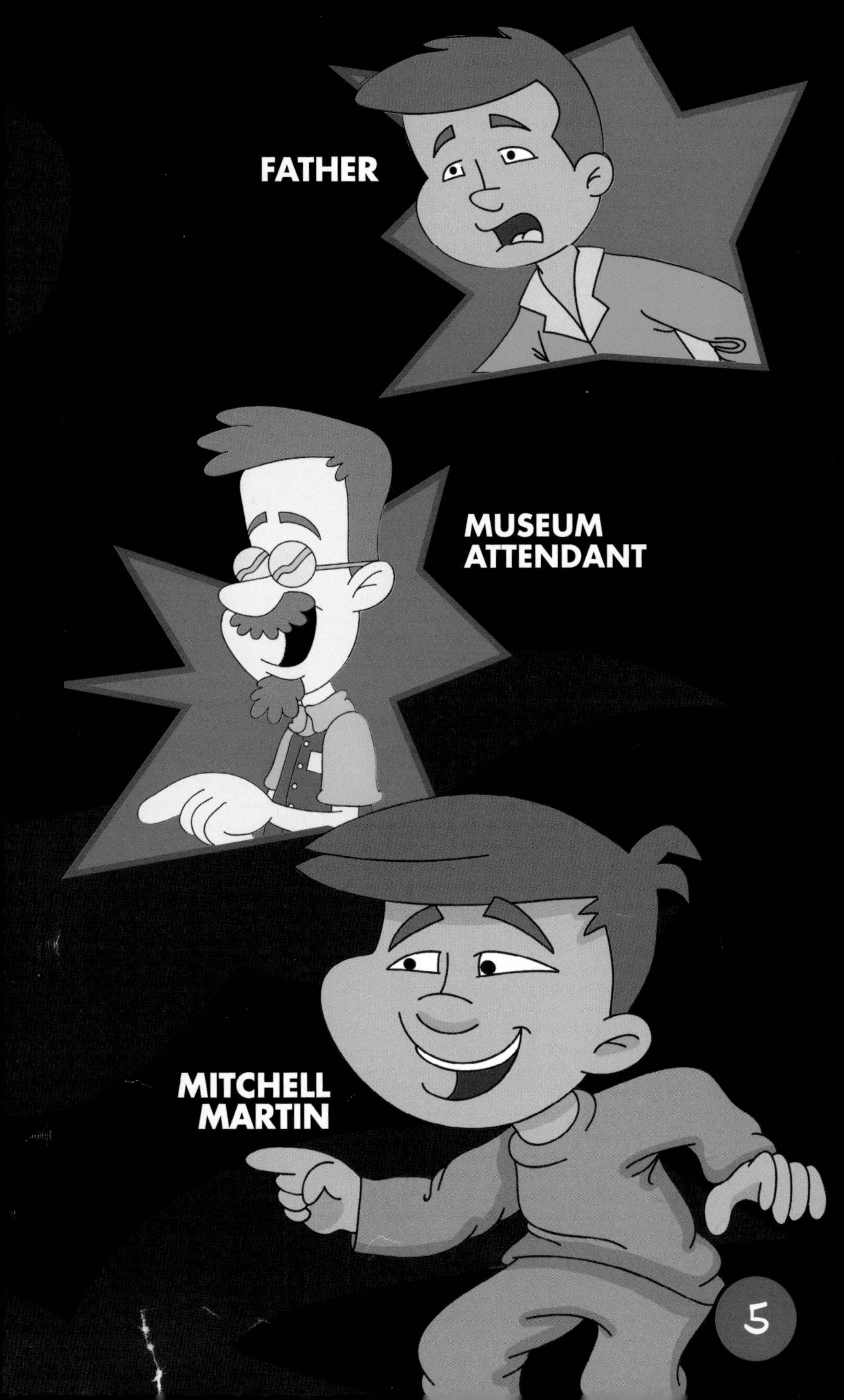
FATHER
MUSEUM ATTENDANT
MITCHELL MARTIN

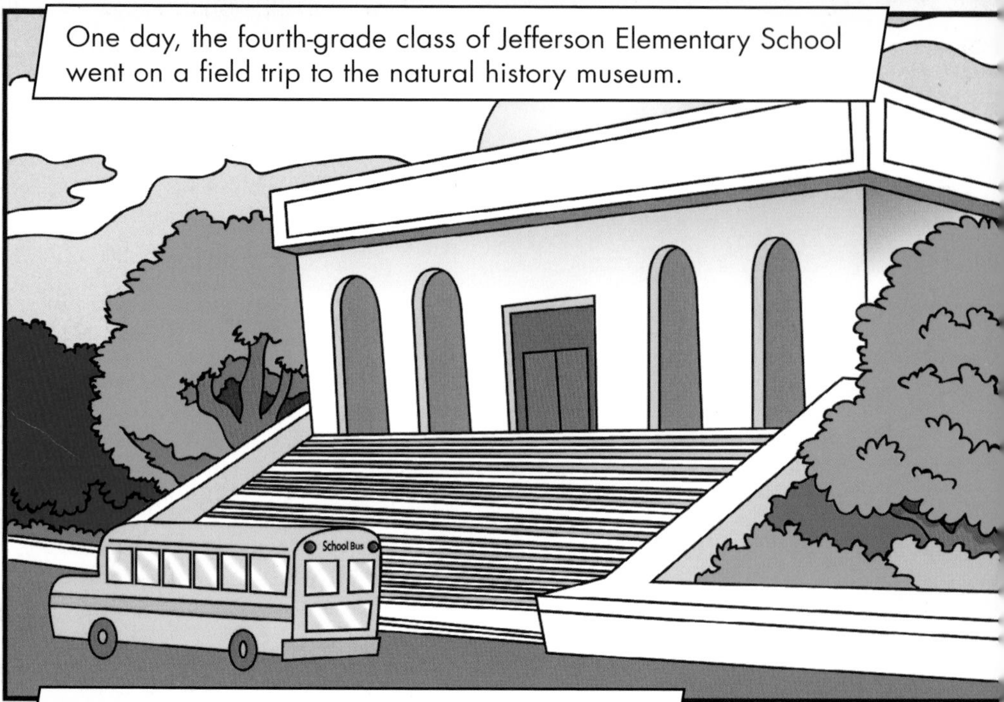
One day, the fourth-grade class of Jefferson Elementary School went on a field trip to the natural history museum.
School Bus

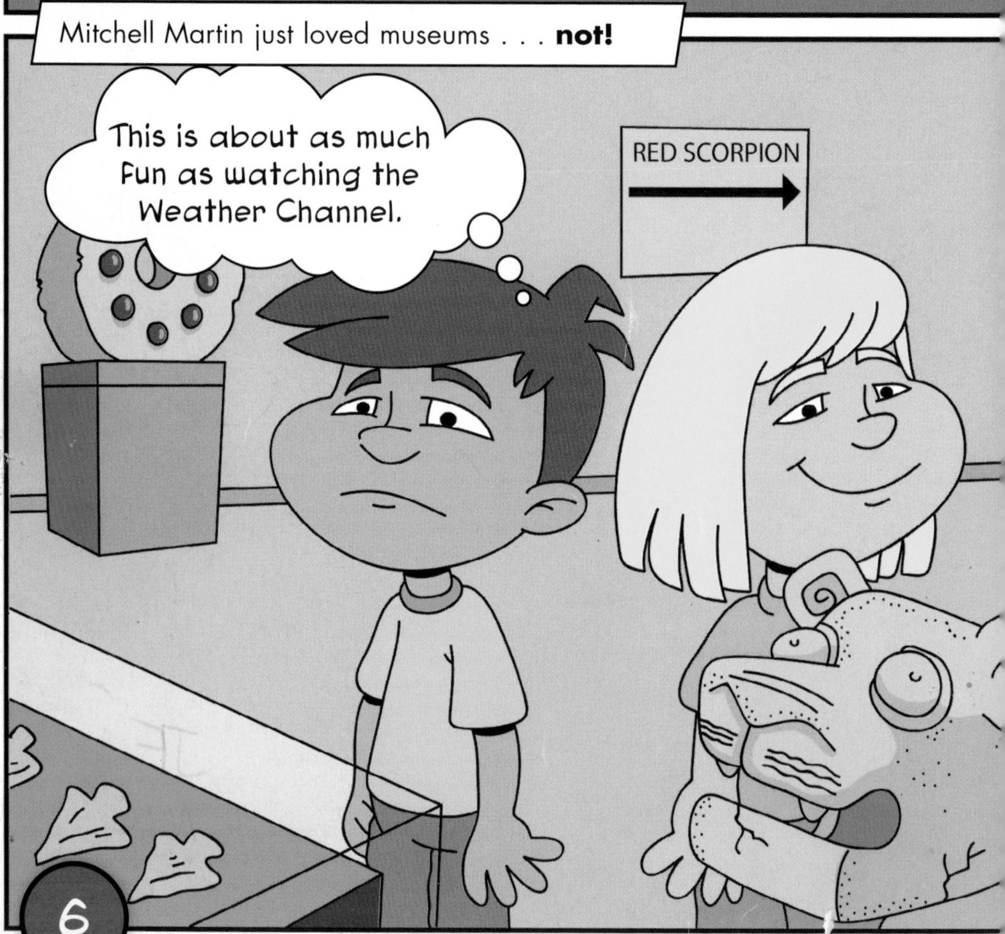
Mitchell Martin just loved museums . . . **not!**
This is about as much fun as watching the Weather Channel.
RED SCORPION

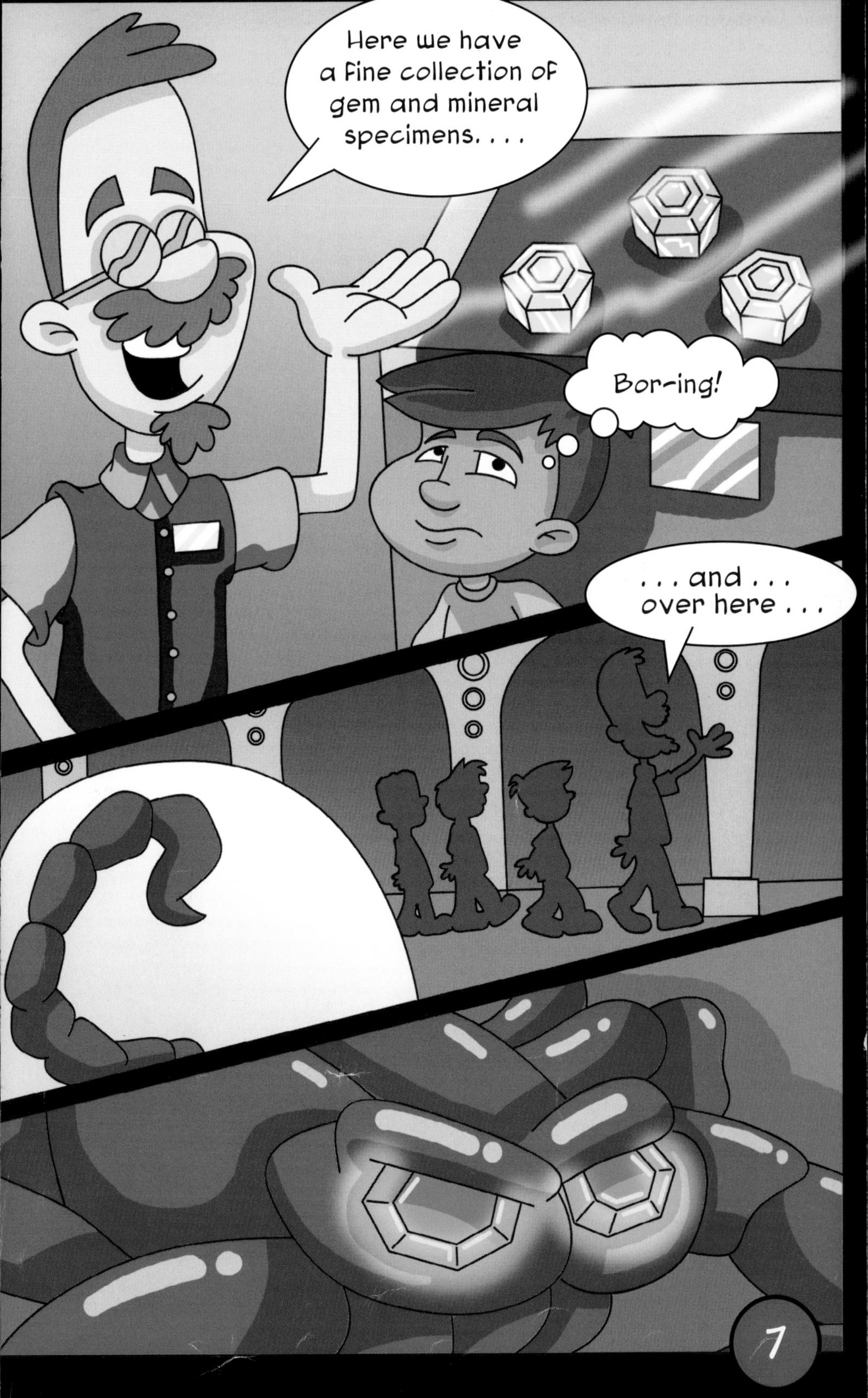
Here we have a fine collection of gem and mineral specimens. . . .
Bor-ing!
. . . and . . . over here . . .

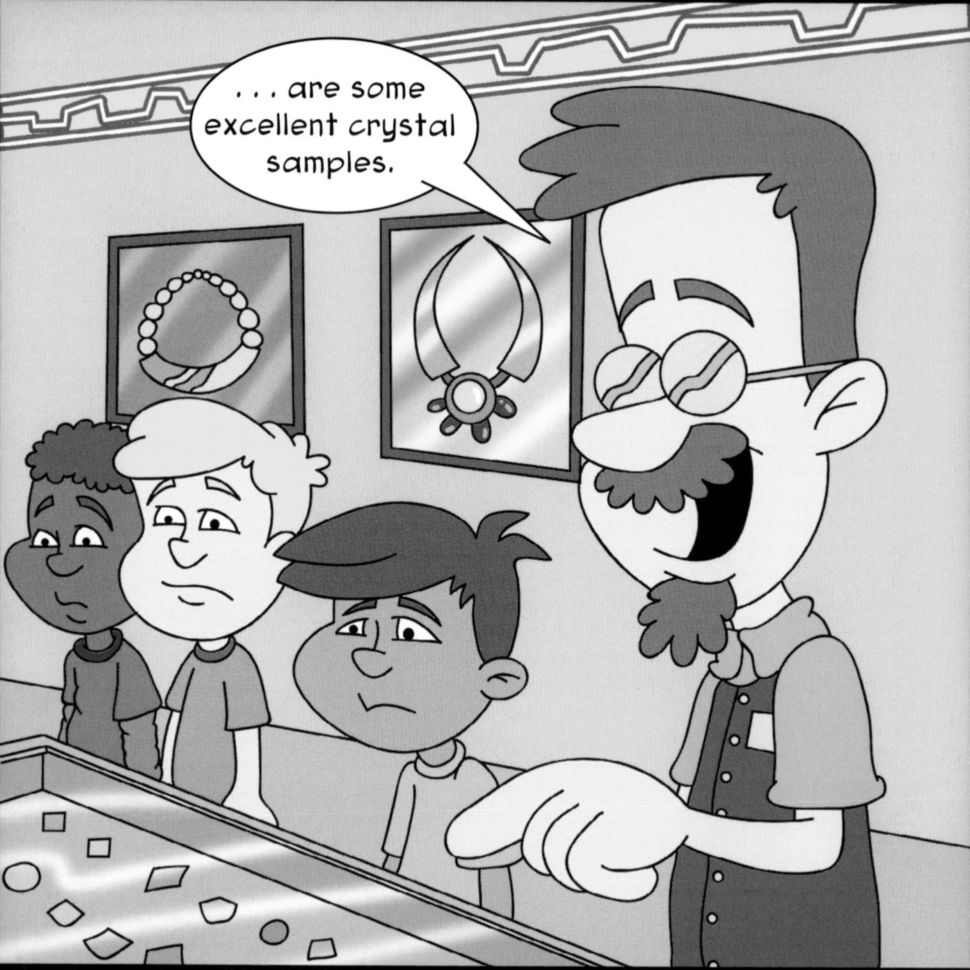
. . . are some excellent crystal samples.

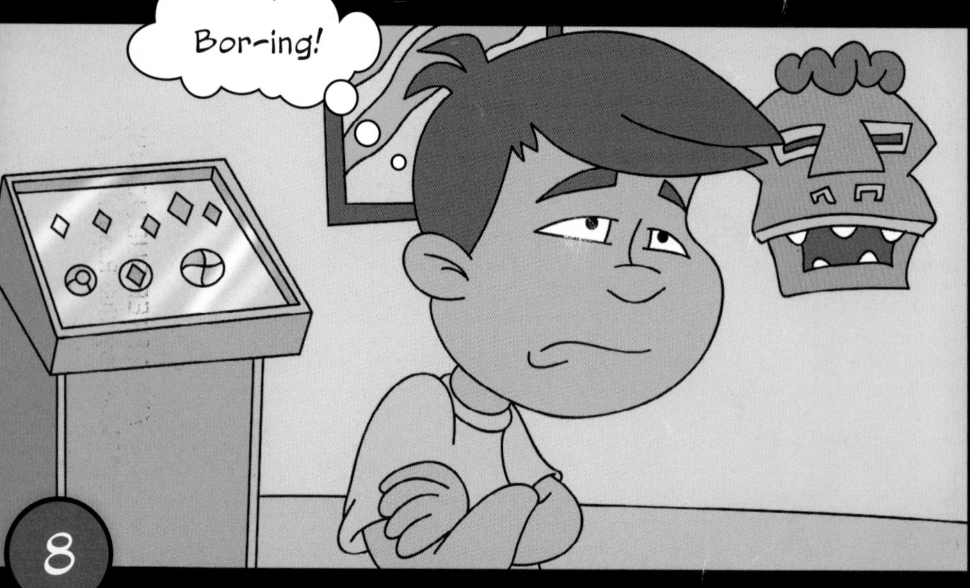
Bor-ing!

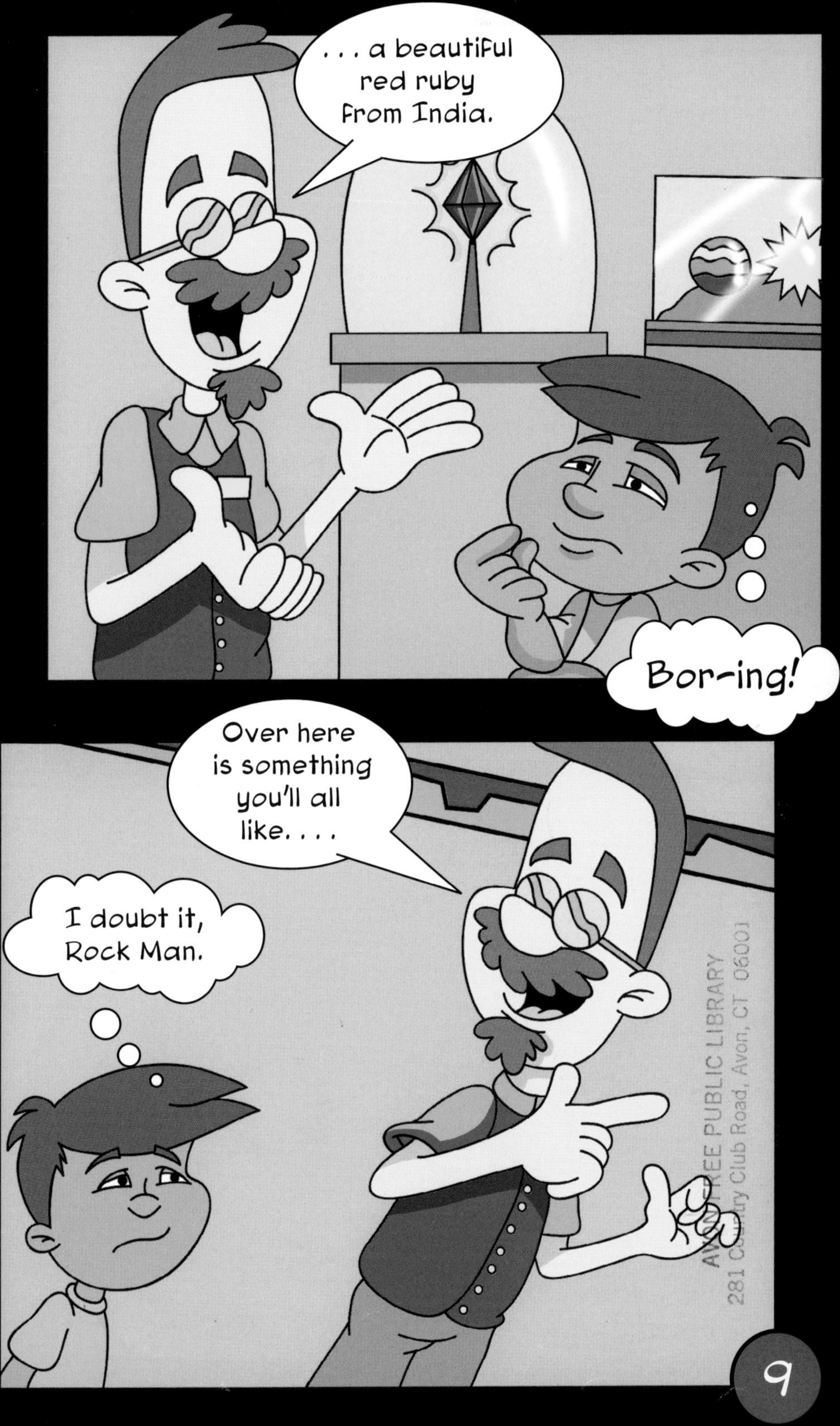
. . . a beautiful red ruby from India.
Bor-ing!
Over here is something you'll all like. . . .
I doubt it, Rock Man.

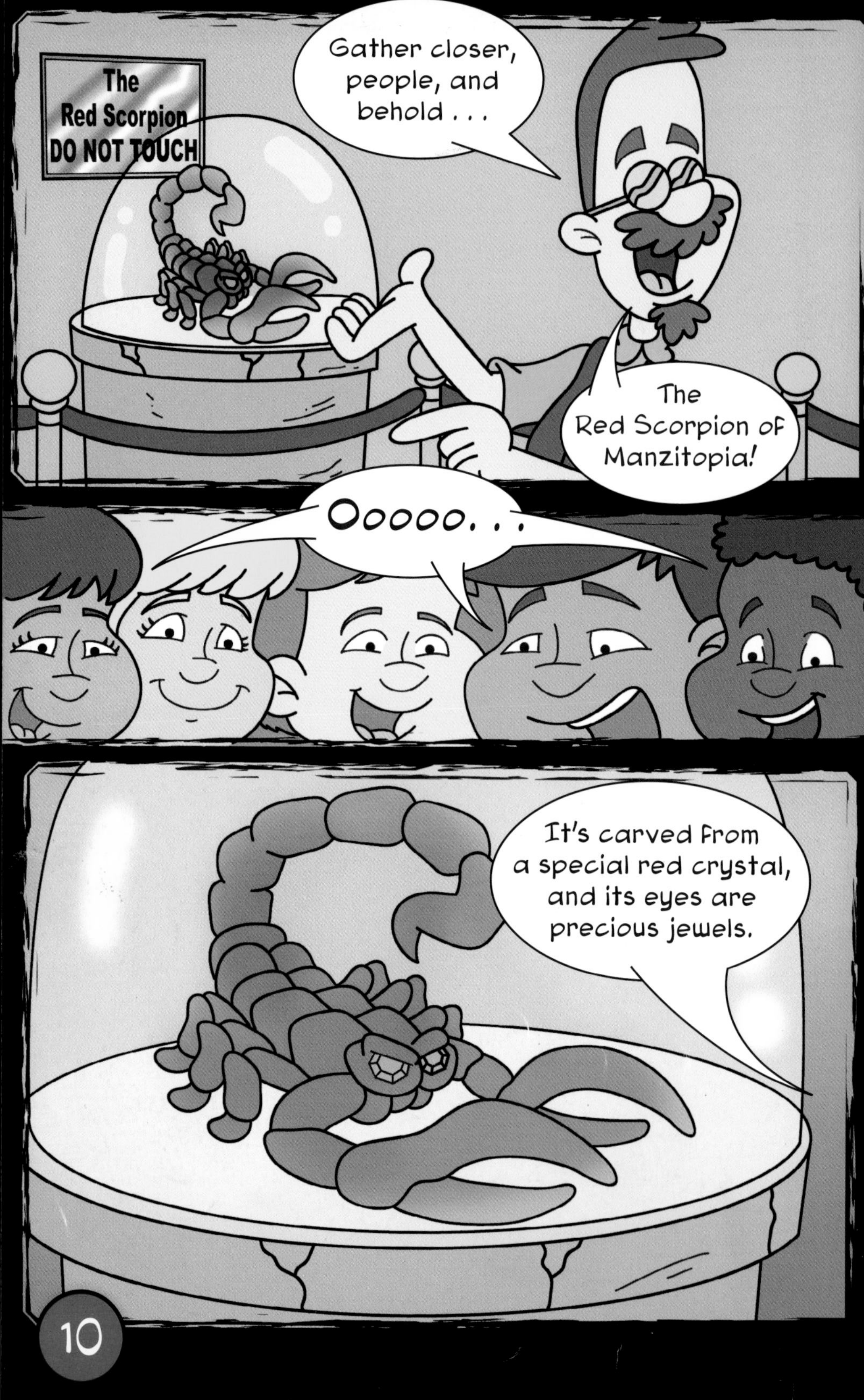

The Red Scorpion DO NOT TOUCH
Gather closer, people, and behold . . .
The Red Scorpion of Manzitopia!
Ooooo. . .
It's carved from a special red crystal, and its eyes are precious jewels.

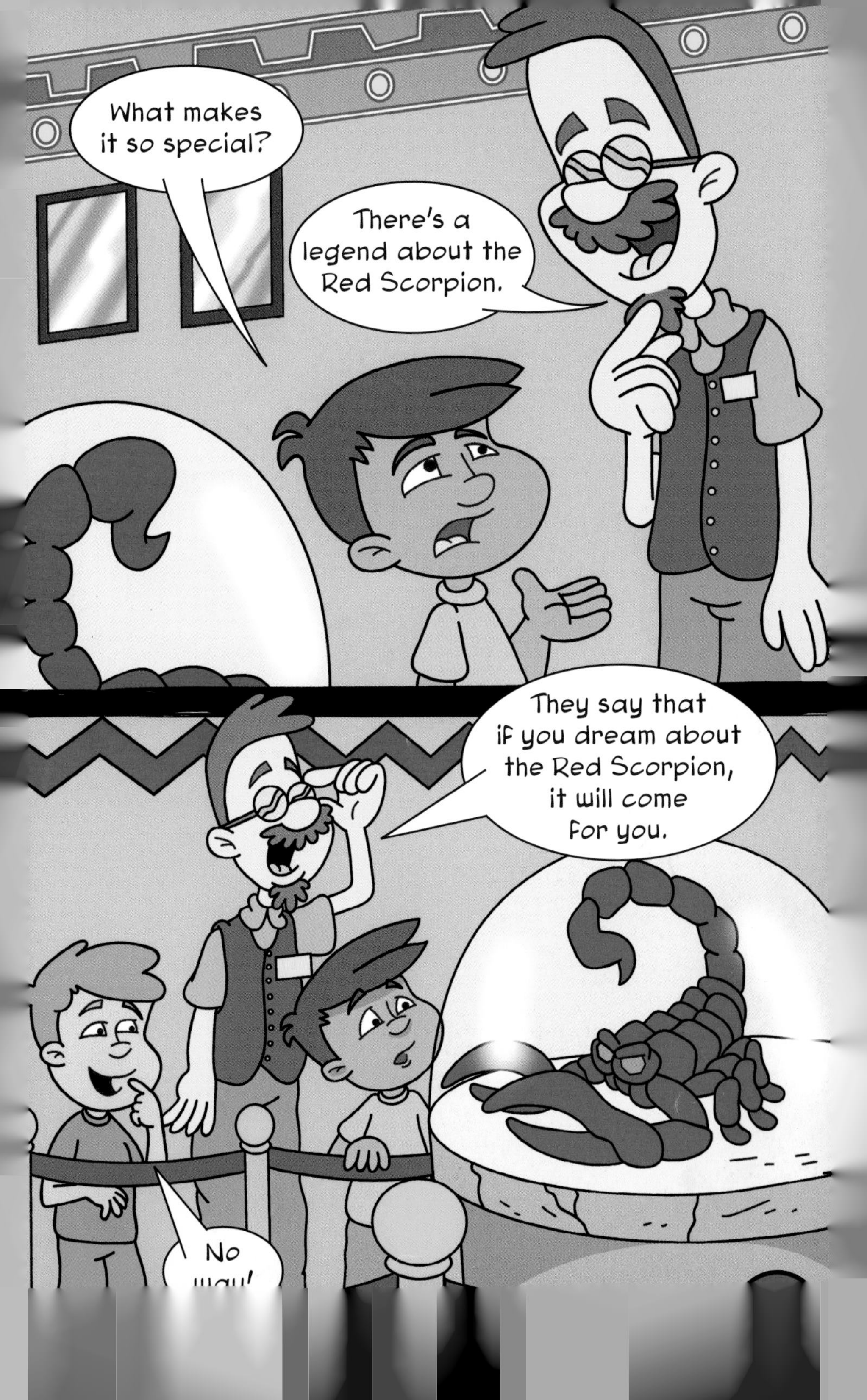

What makes it so special?
There's a legend about the Red Scorpion.
They say that if you dream about the Red Scorpion, it will come for you.
No

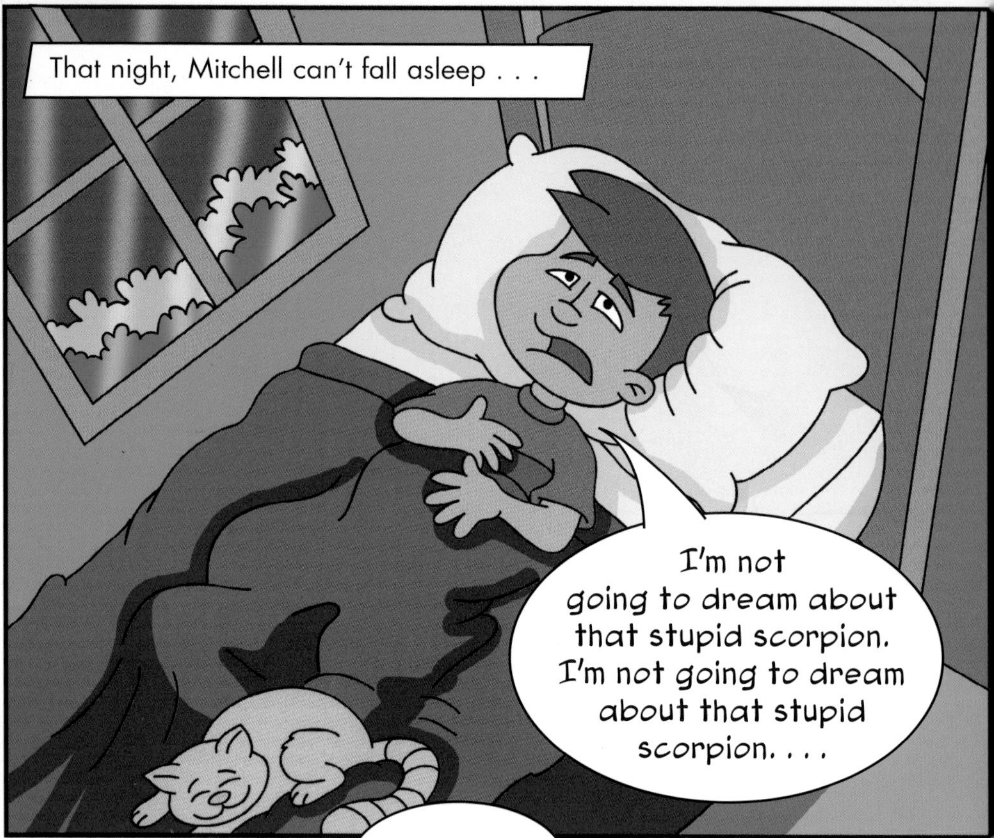
That night, Mitchell can't fall asleep . . .
I'm not going to dream about that stupid scorpion. I'm not going to dream about that stupid scorpion. . . .

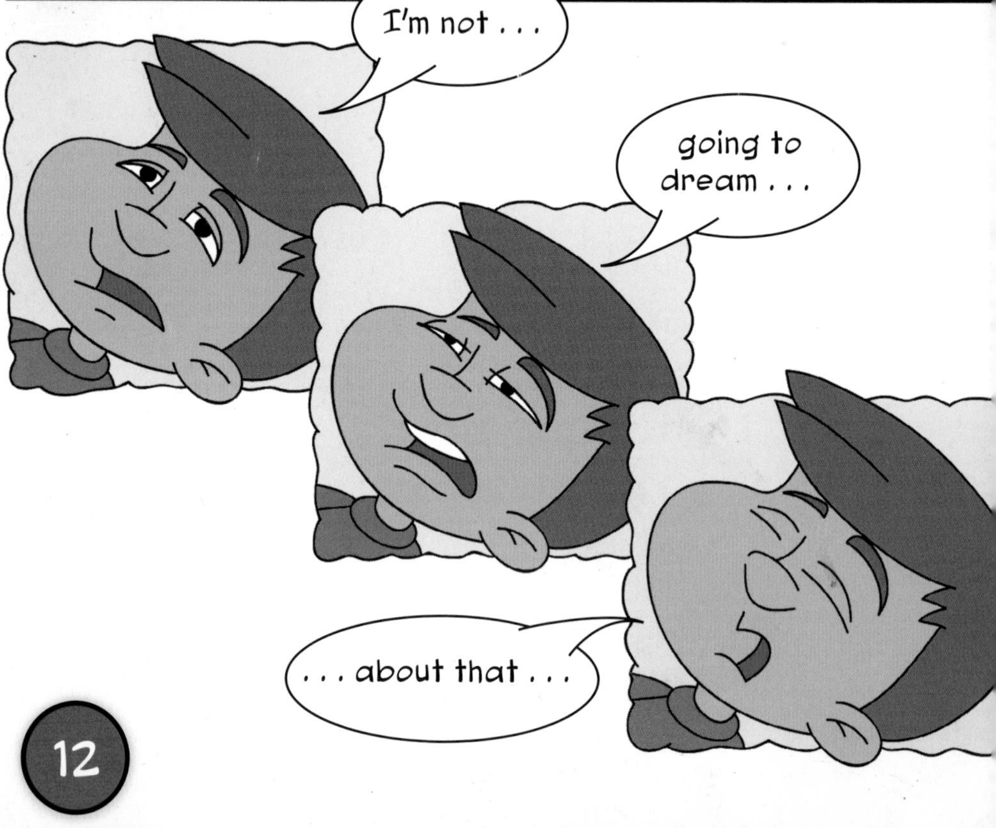
I'm not . . .
going to dream . . .
. . . about that . . .

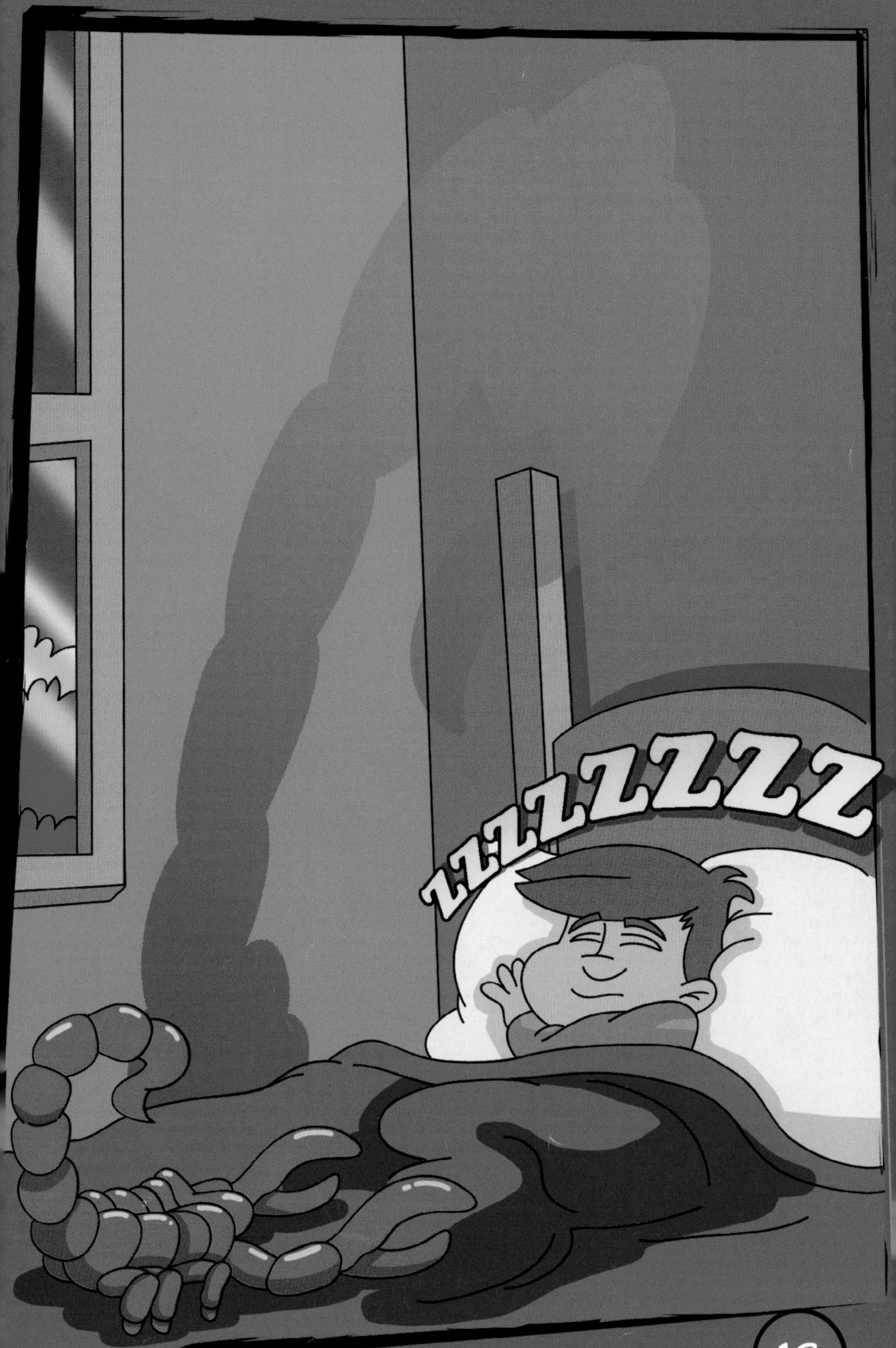
ZZZZZZZZZZ

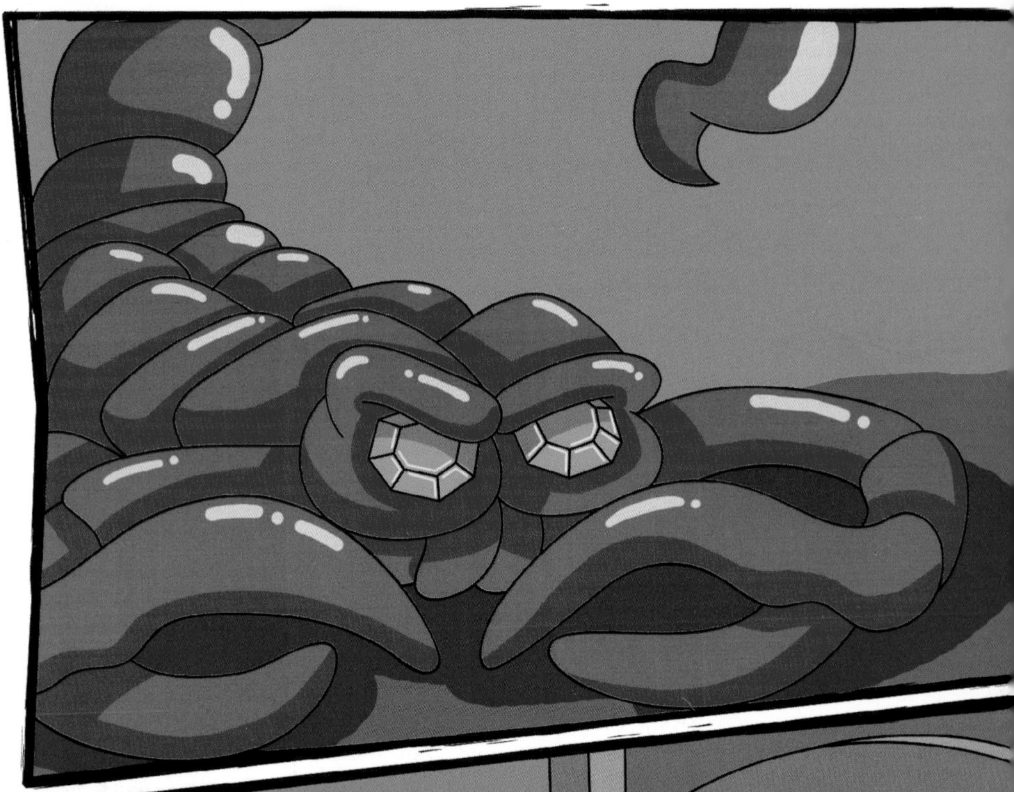

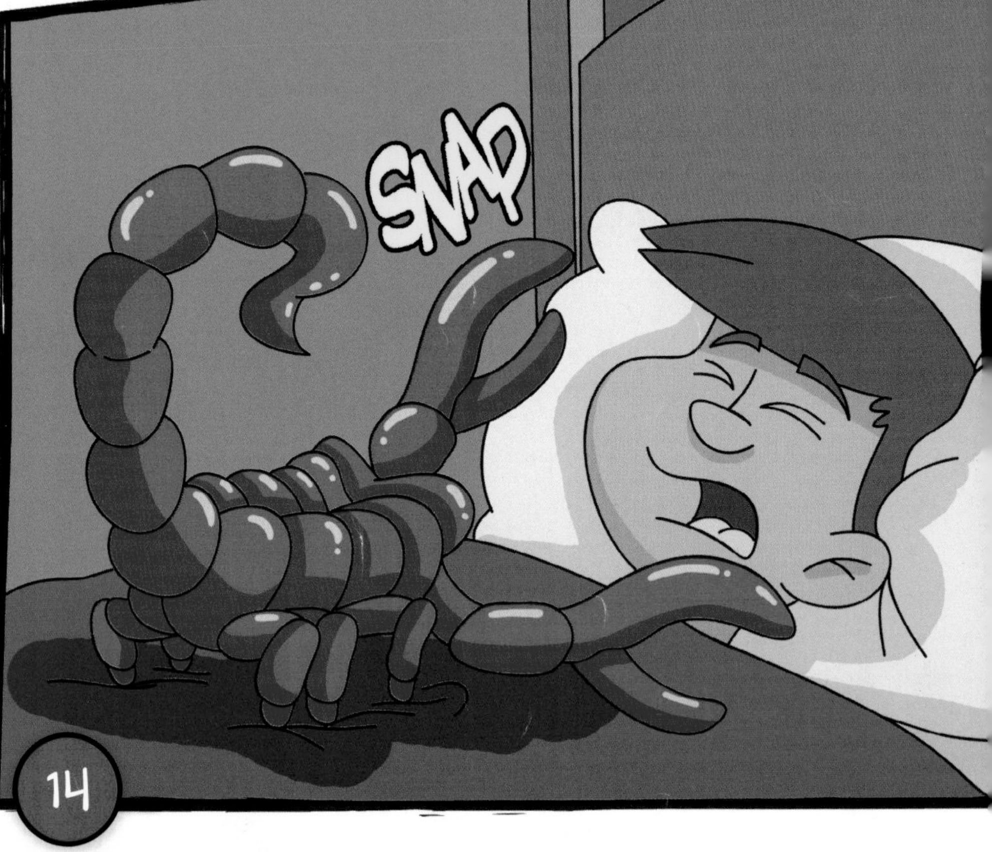
SNAP

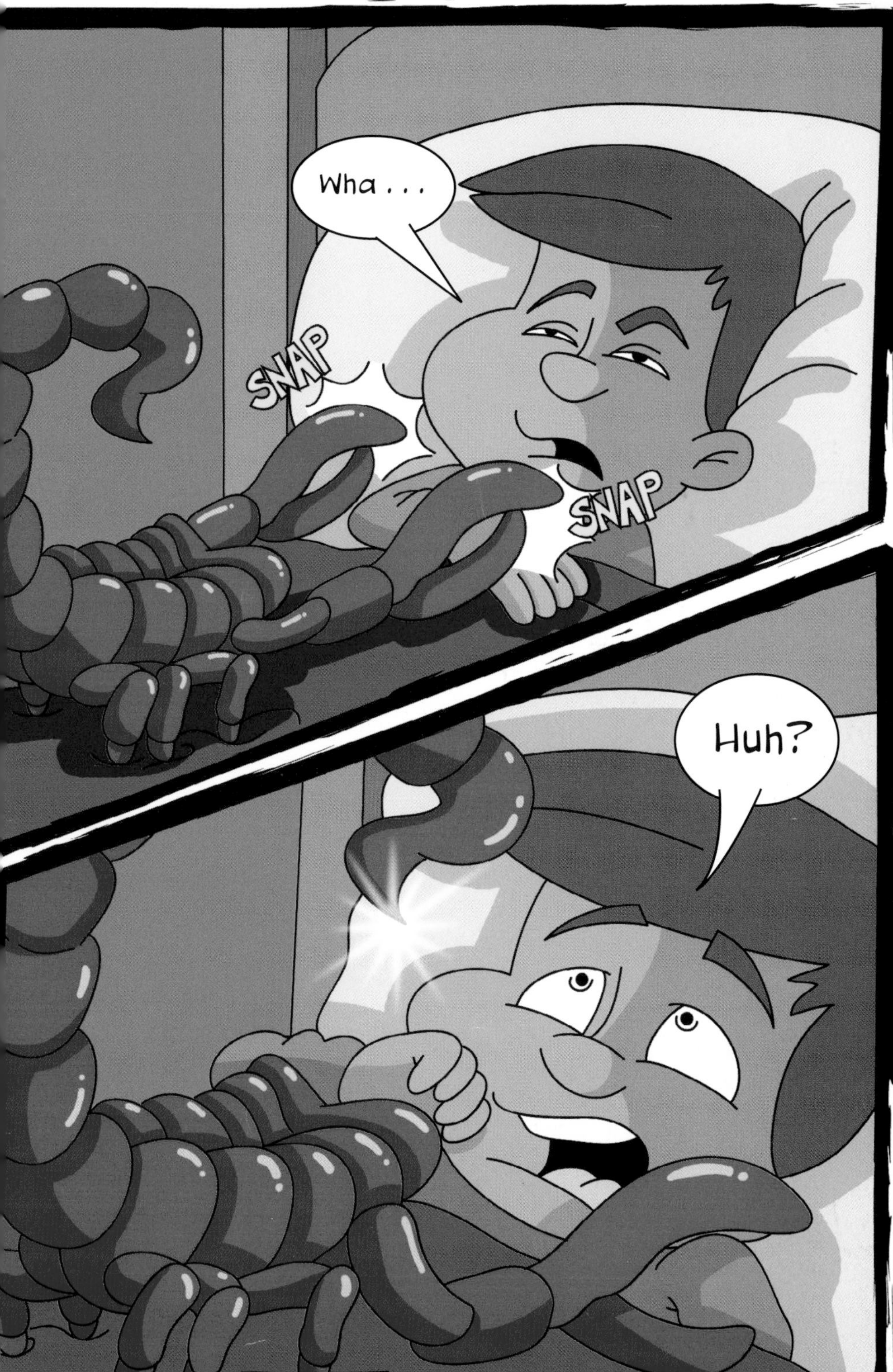
Wha . . .
SNAP
SNAP
Huh?

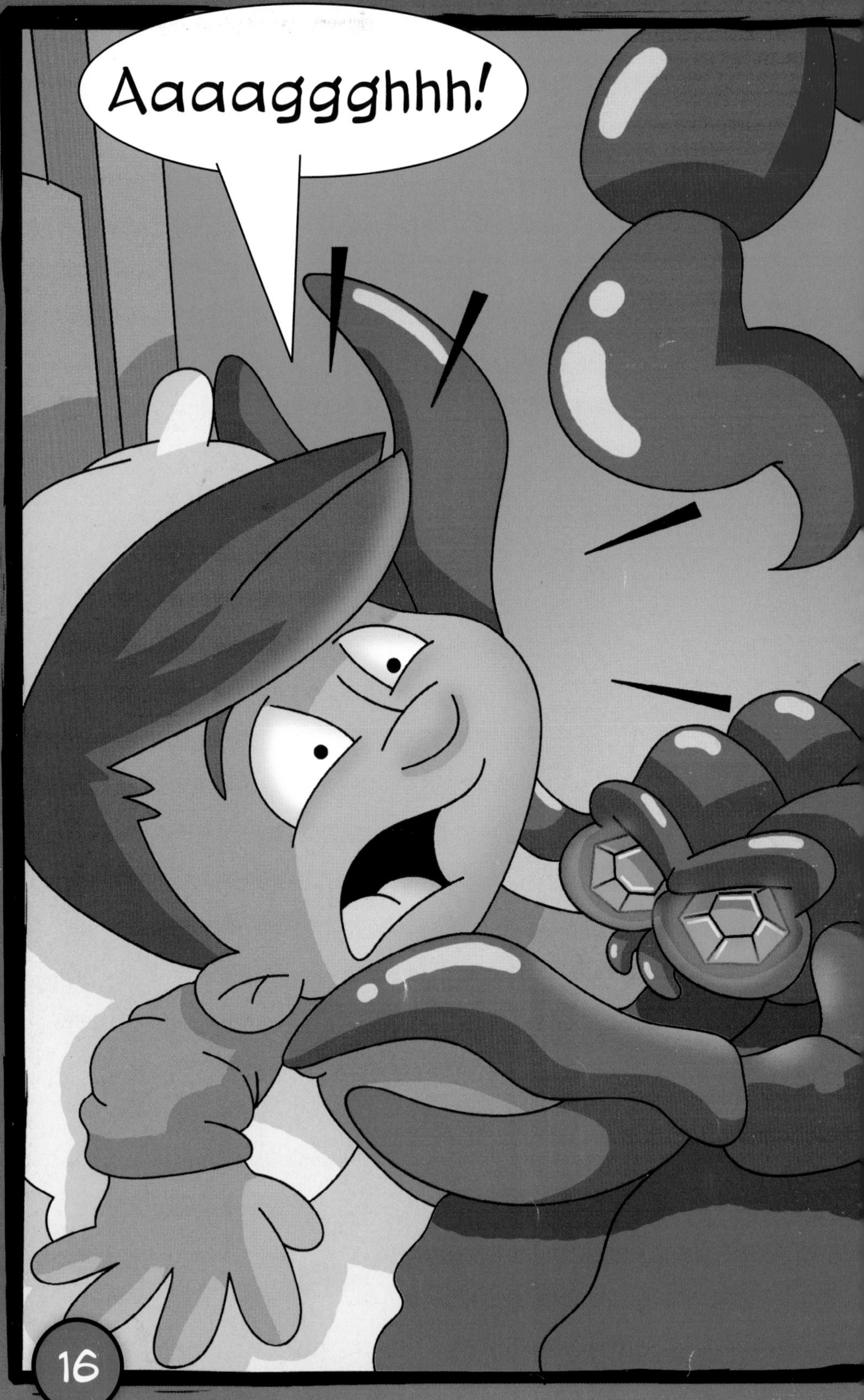
Aaaaagghhh!

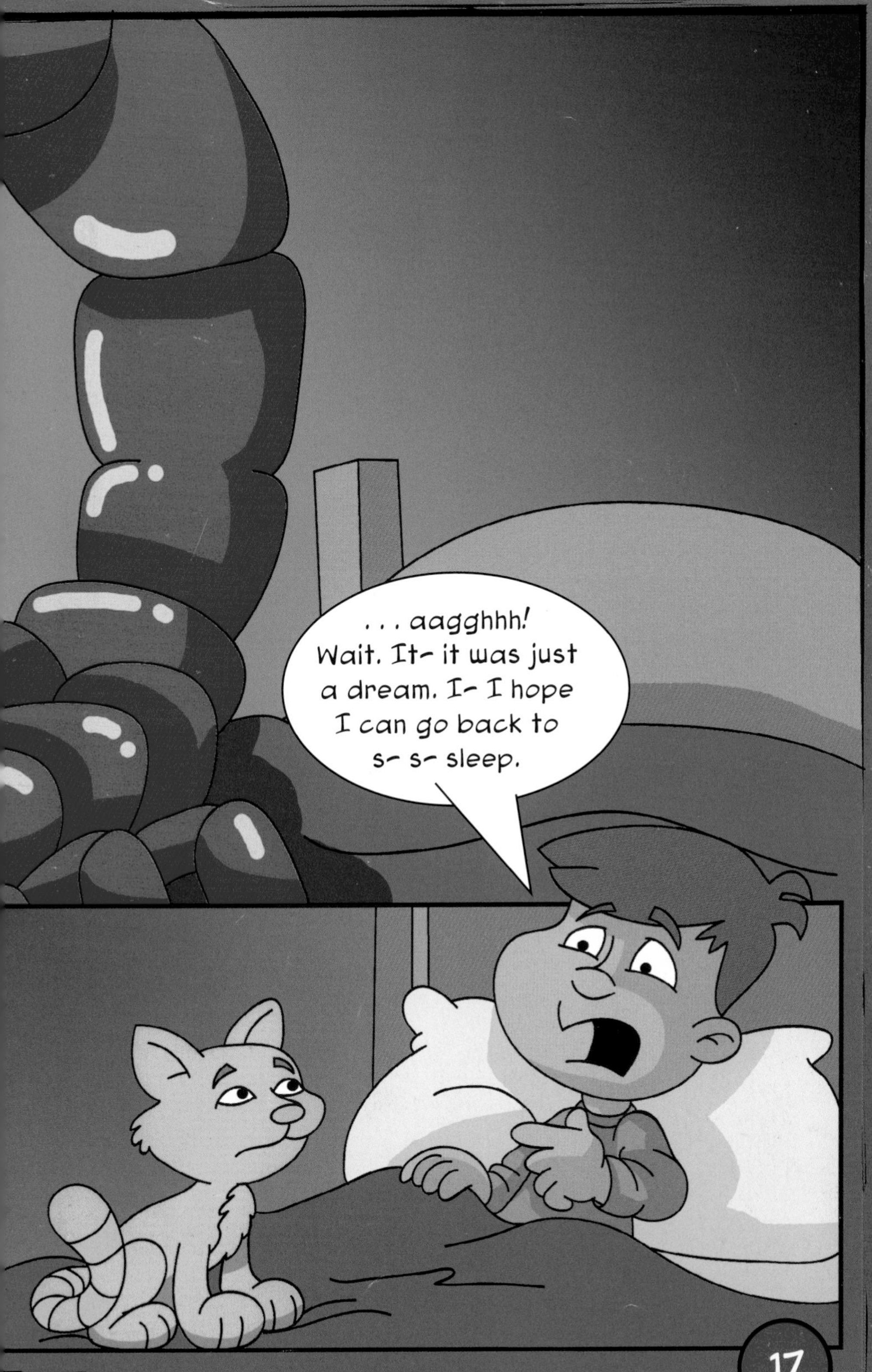
. . . aagghhh! Wait. It- it was just a dream. I- I hope I can go back to s- s- sleep.

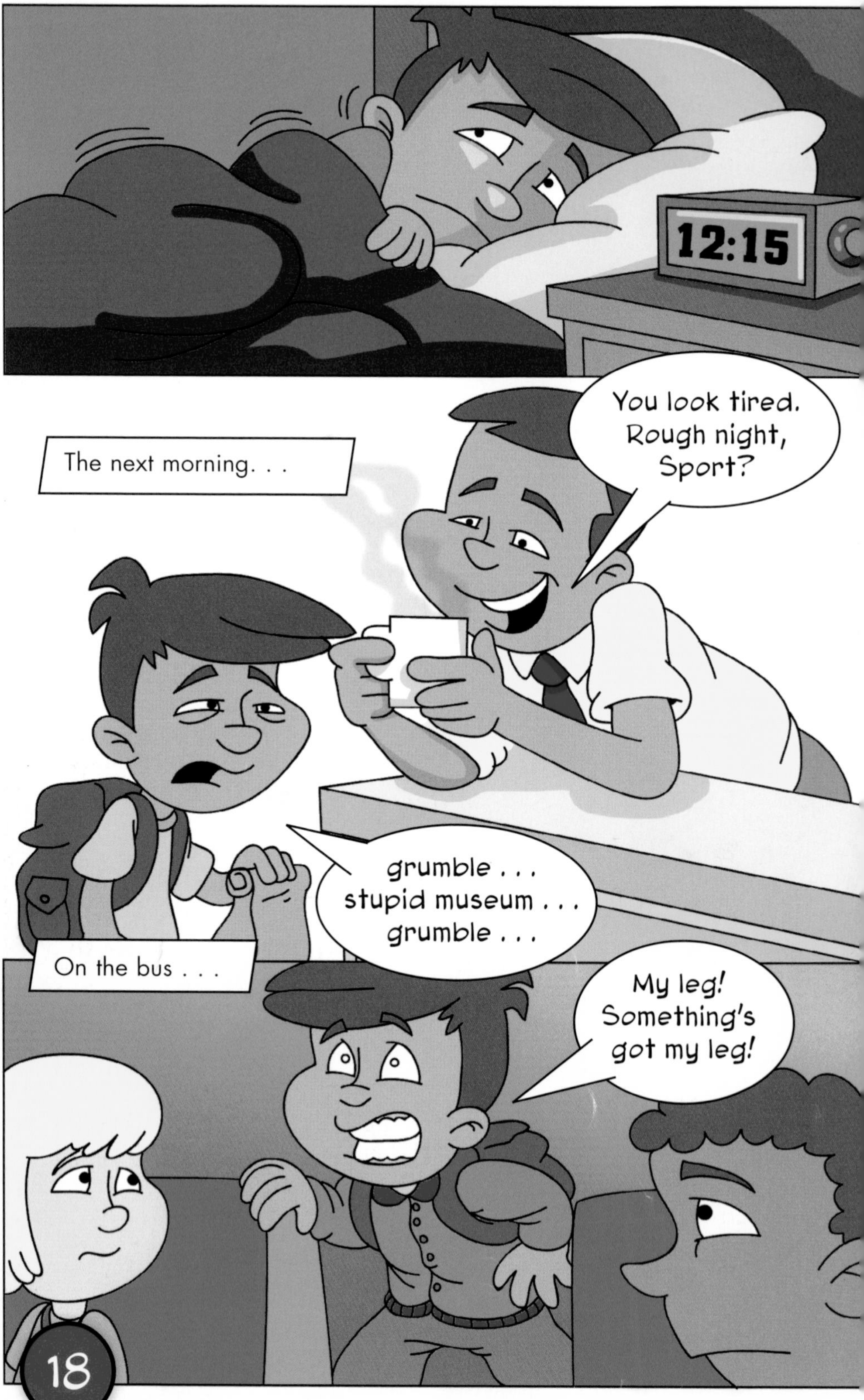
12:15
The next morning. . .
You look tired. Rough night, Sport?
grumble . . . stupid museum . . . grumble . . .
On the bus . . .
My leg! Something's got my leg!

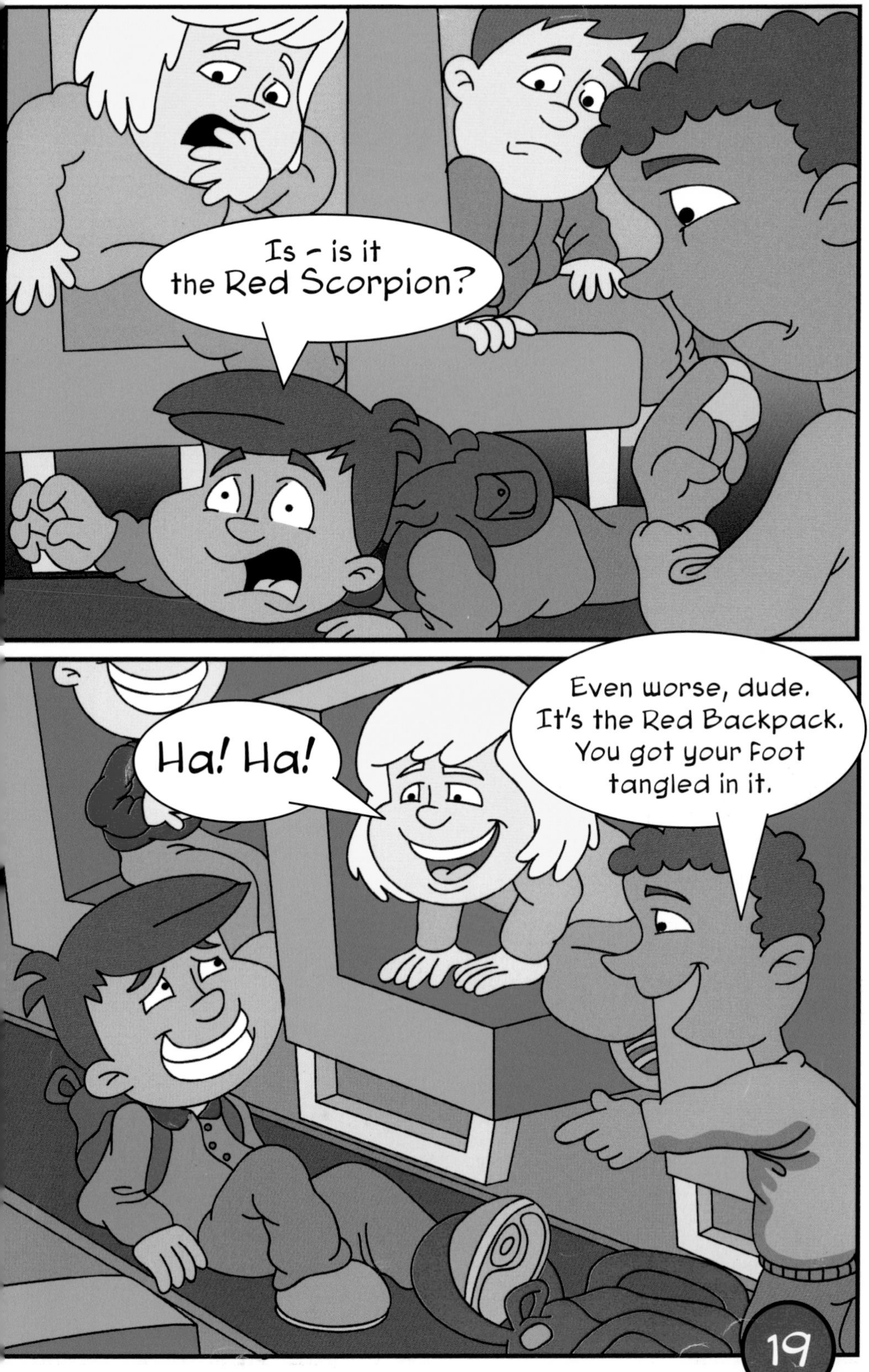
Is - is it the Red Scorpion?
Ha! Ha!
Even worse, dude. It's the Red Backpack. You got your foot tangled in it.

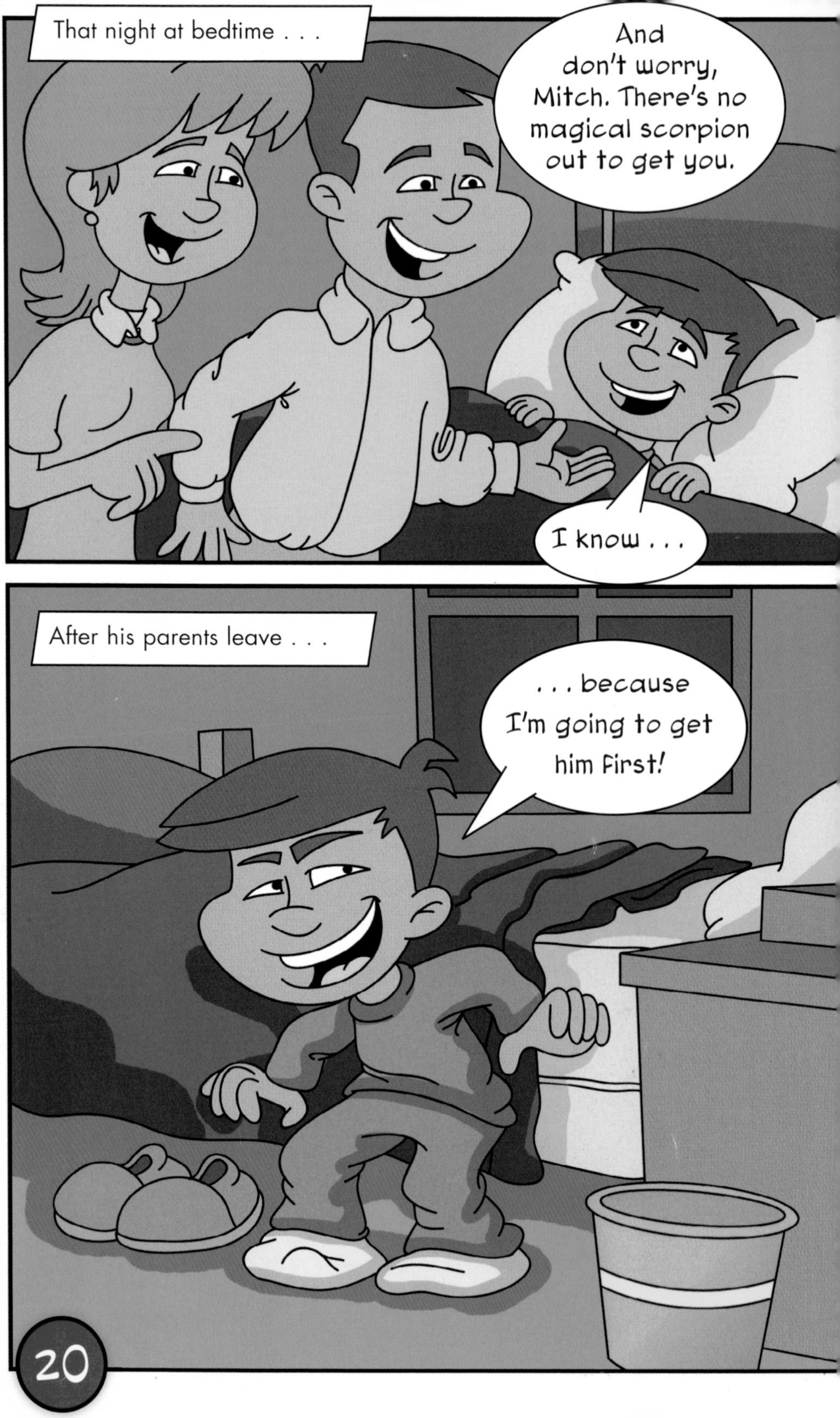
That night at bedtime . . .
And don't worry, Mitch. There's no magical scorpion out to get you.
I know . . .
After his parents leave . . .
. . . because I'm going to get him first!

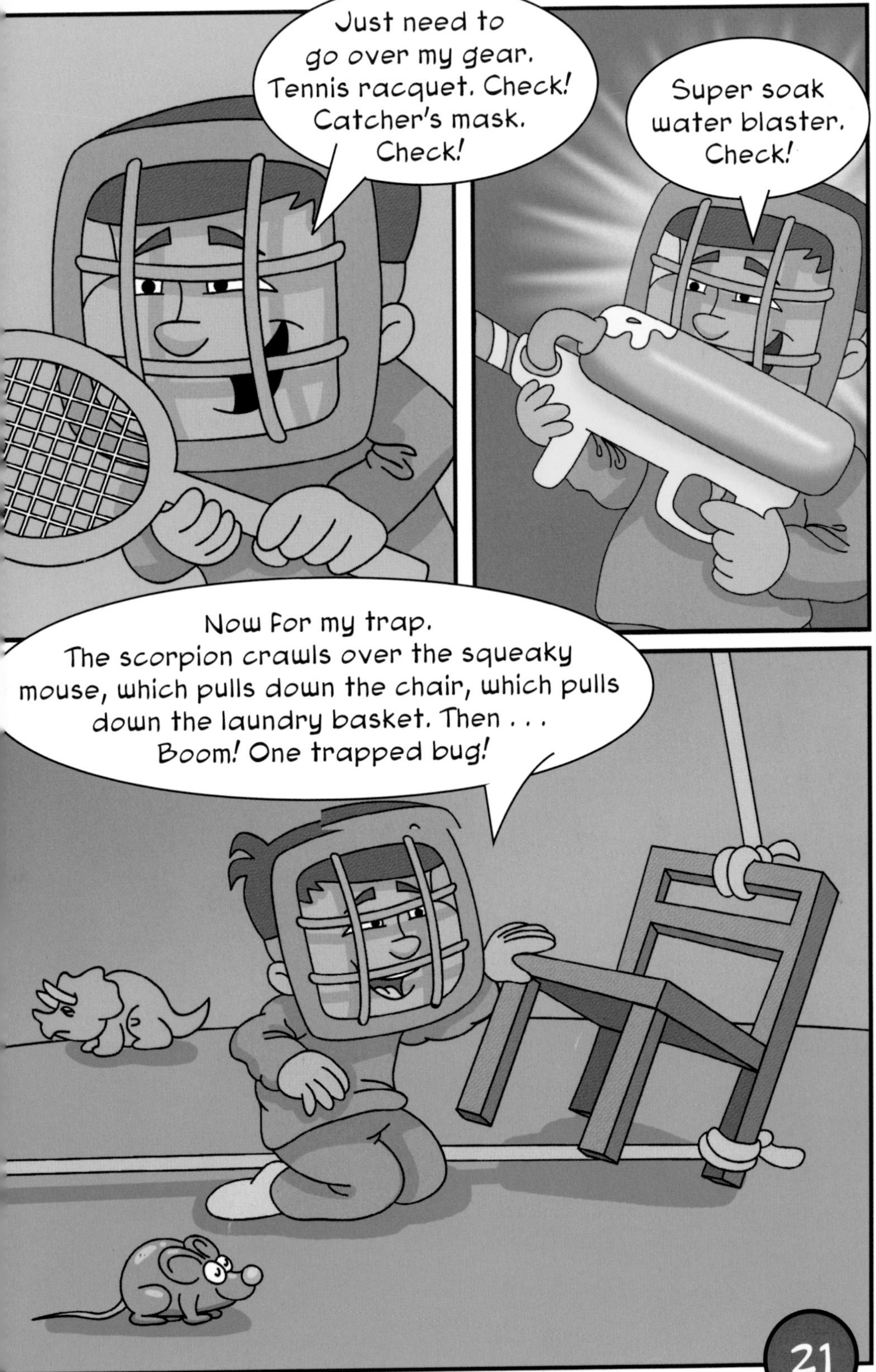
Just need to go over my gear. Tennis racquet. Check! Catcher's mask. Check!
Super soak water blaster. Check!
Now for my trap. The scorpion crawls over the squeaky mouse, which pulls down the chair, which pulls down the laundry basket. Then . . . Boom! One trapped bug!

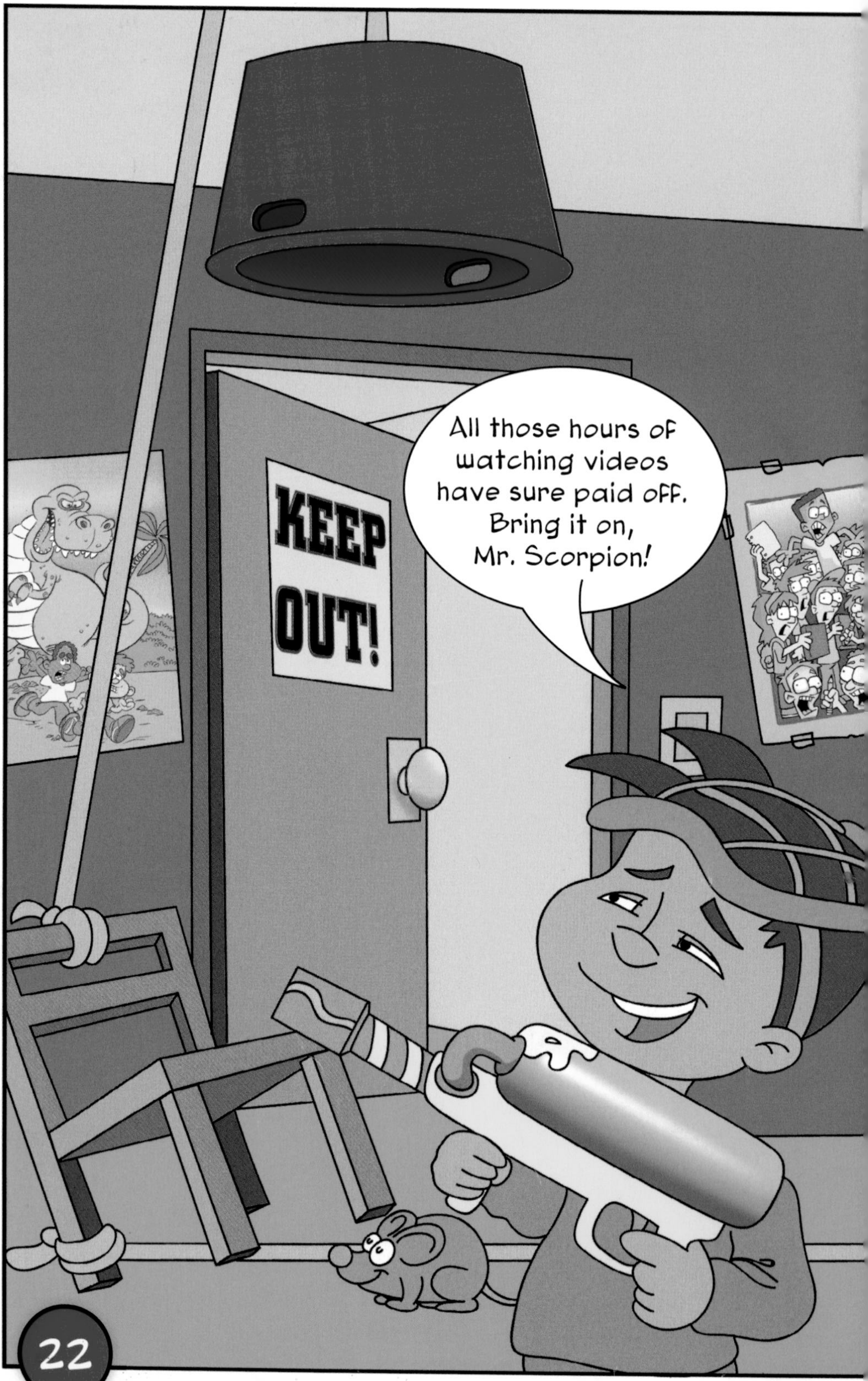
KEEP OUT!
All those hours of watching videos have sure paid off. Bring it on, Mr. Scorpion!

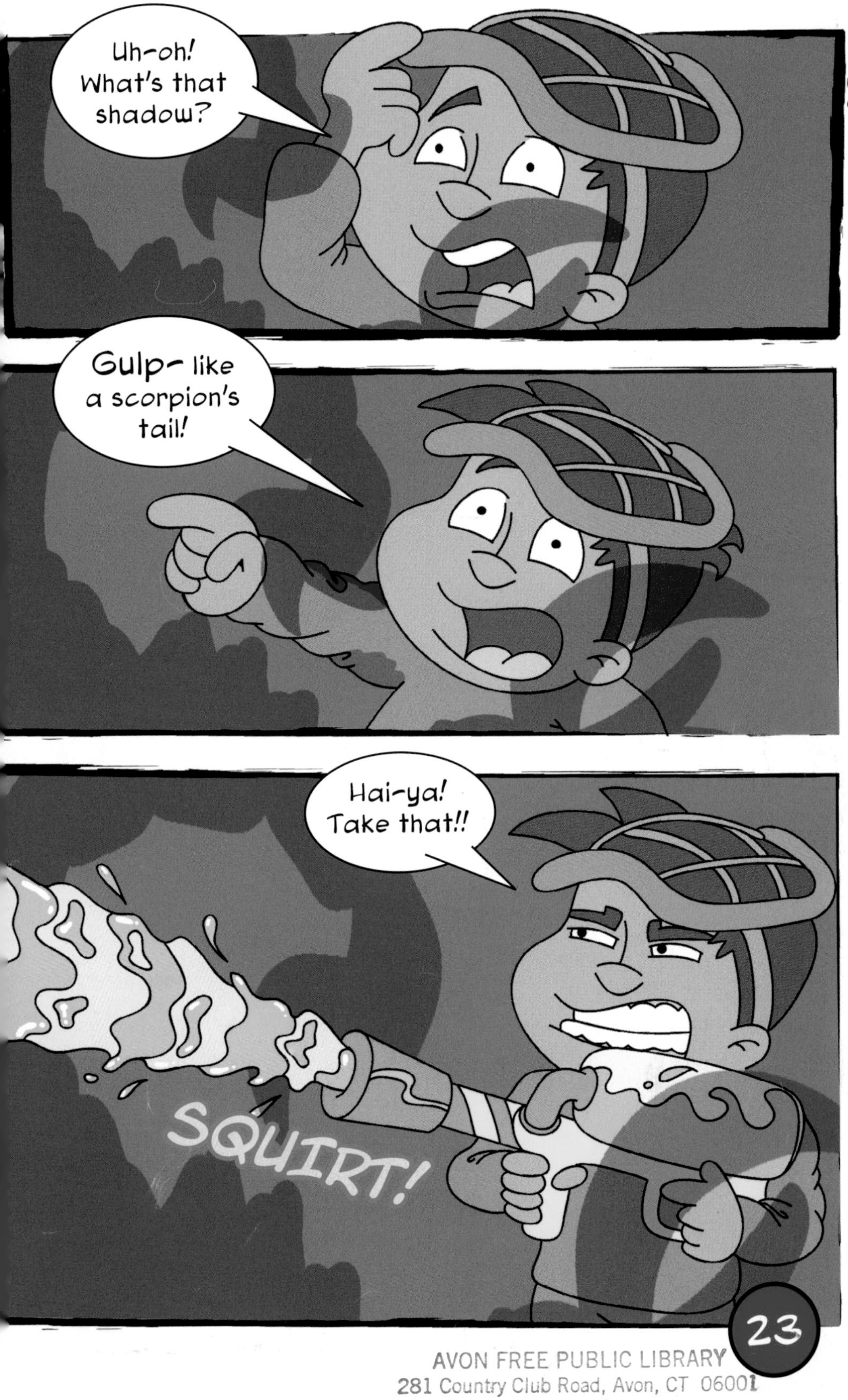
Uh-oh! What's that shadow?
Gulp- like a scorpion's tail!
Hai-ya! Take that!!
SQUIRT!

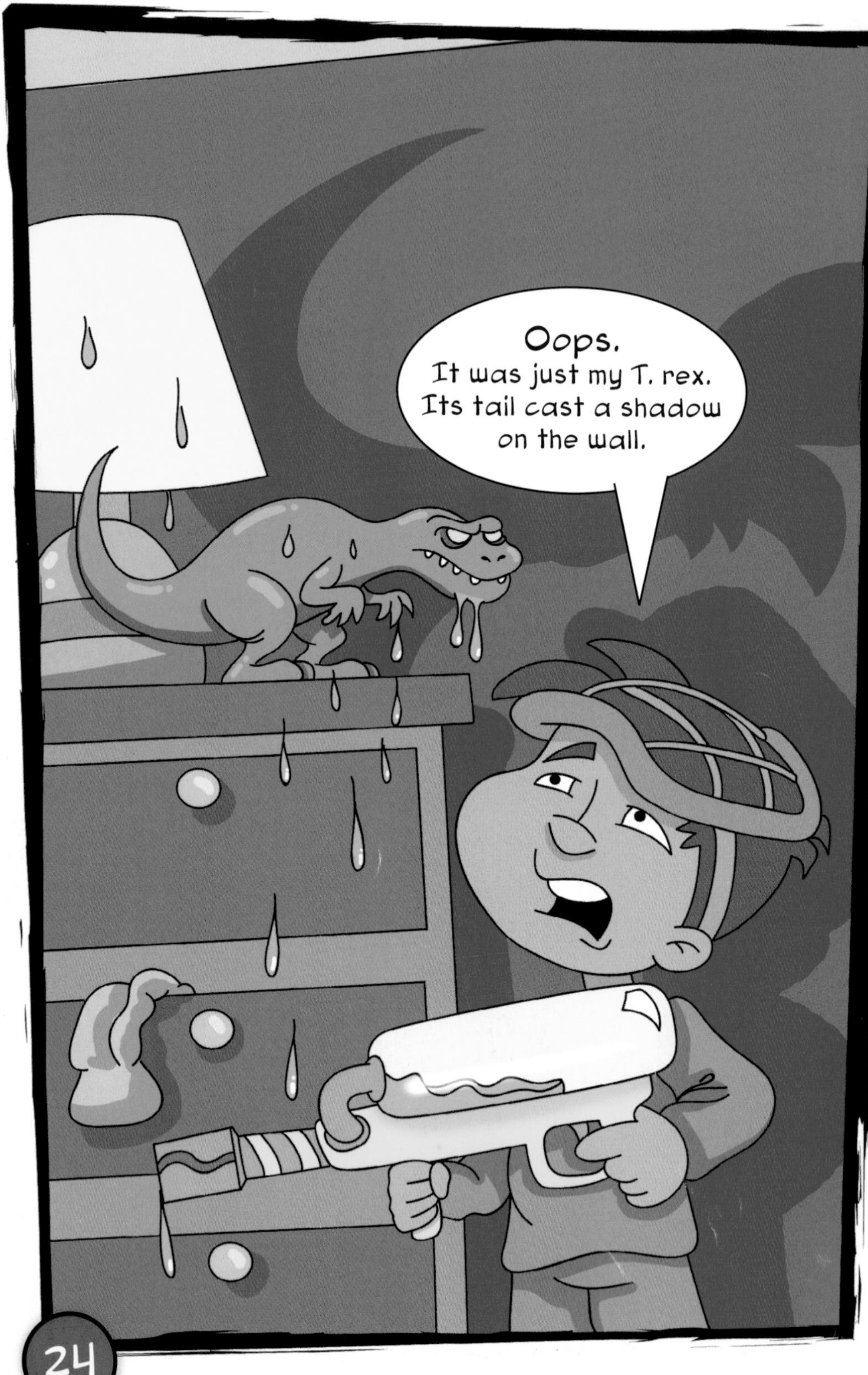
Oops.
It was just my T. rex.
Its tail cast a shadow
on the wall.

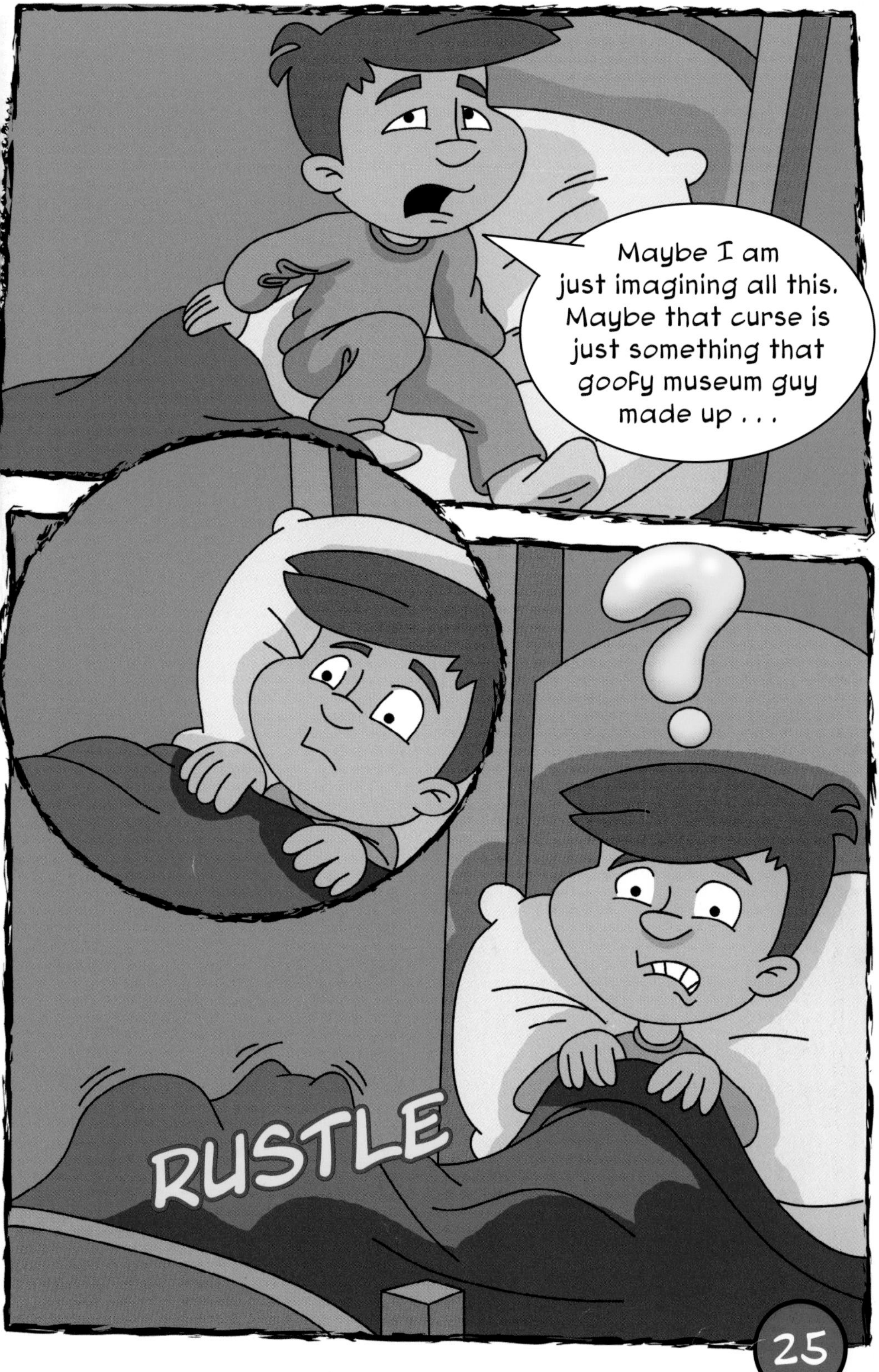
Maybe I am just imagining all this. Maybe that curse is just something that goofy museum guy made up . . .
RUSTLE

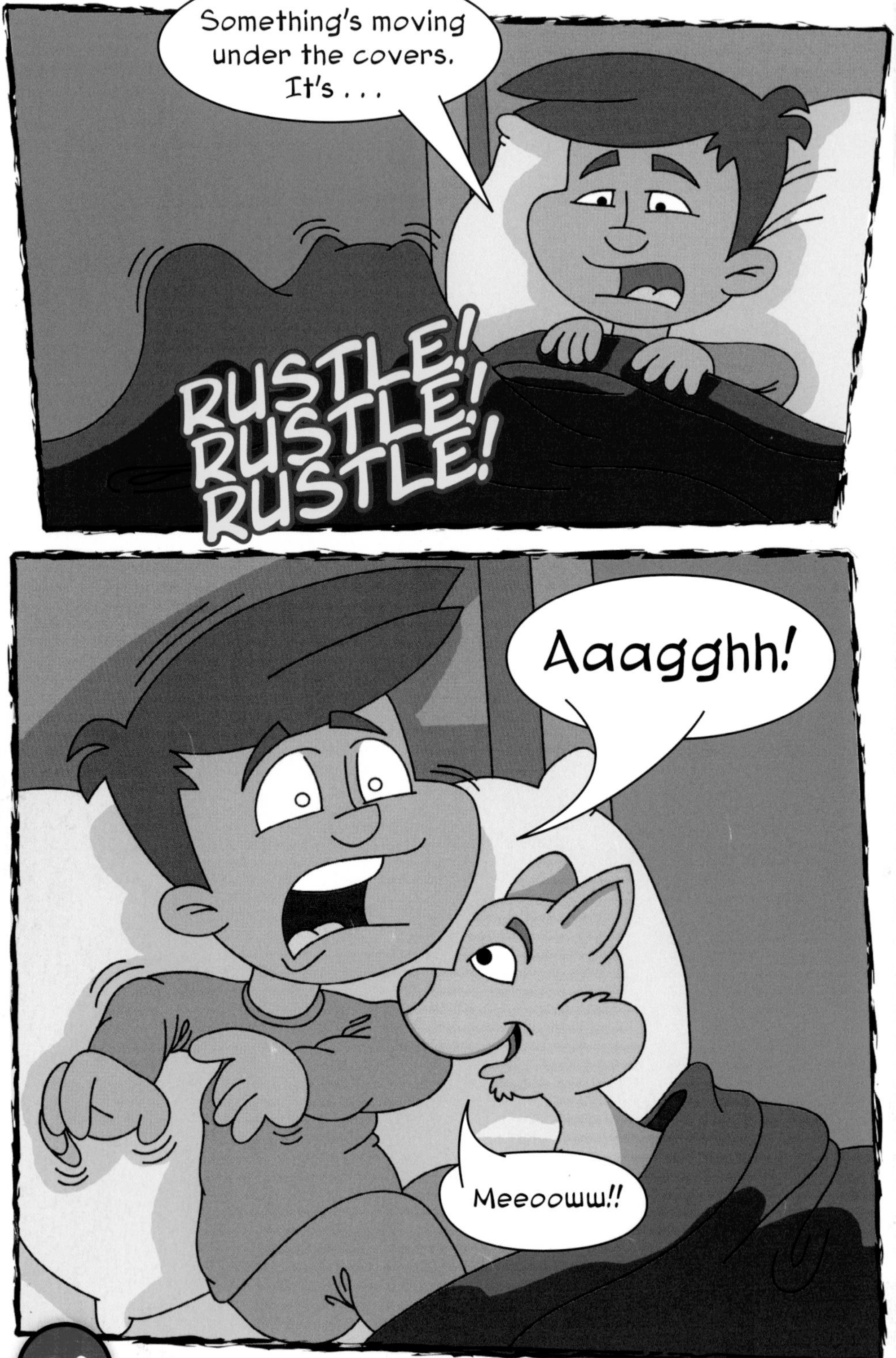
Something's moving under the covers. It's . . .
RUSTLE! RUSTLE! RUSTLE!
Aaagghh!
Meeooww!!

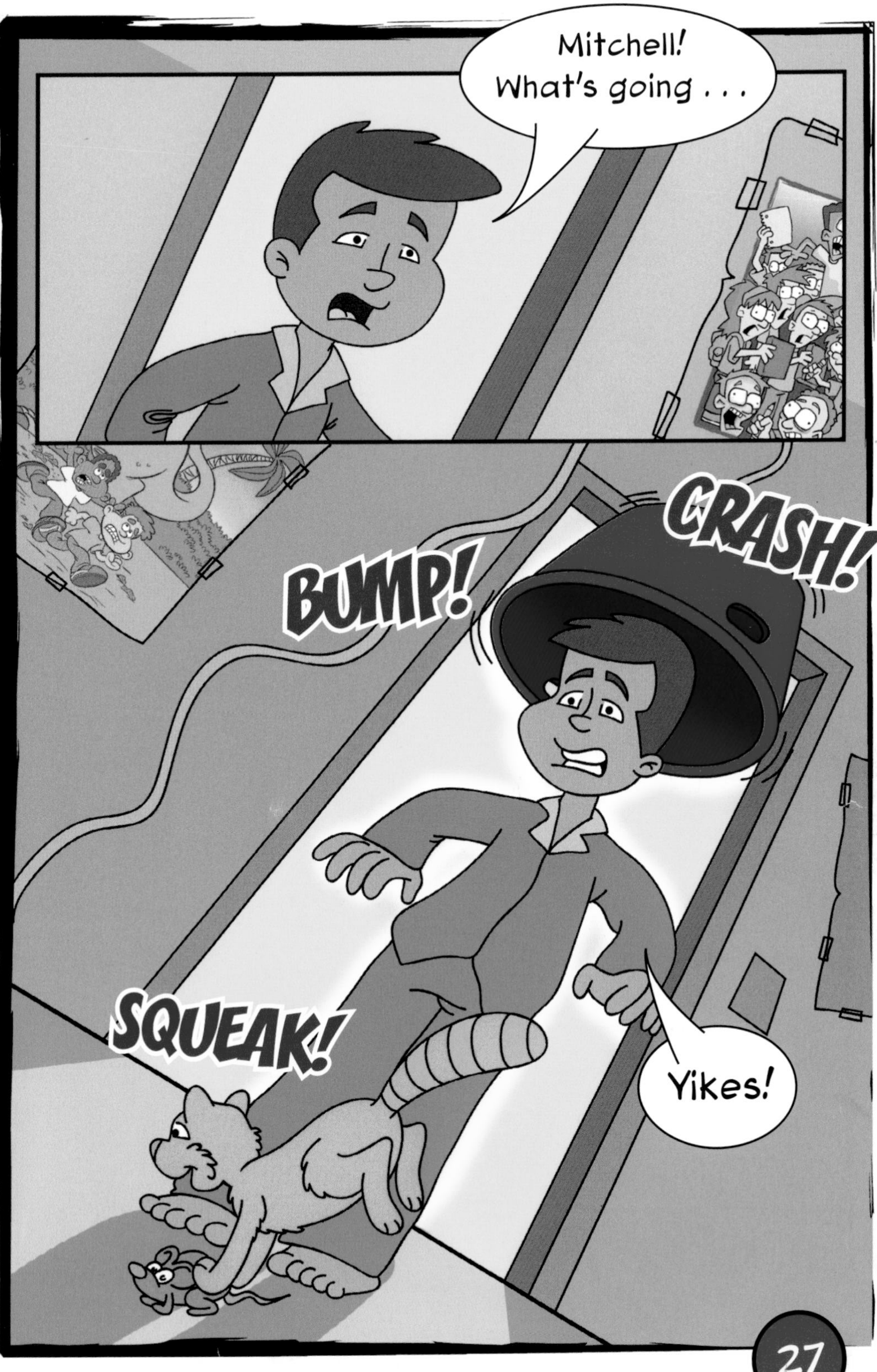
Mitchell! What's going . . .
CRASH!
BUMP!
SQUEAK!
Yikes!

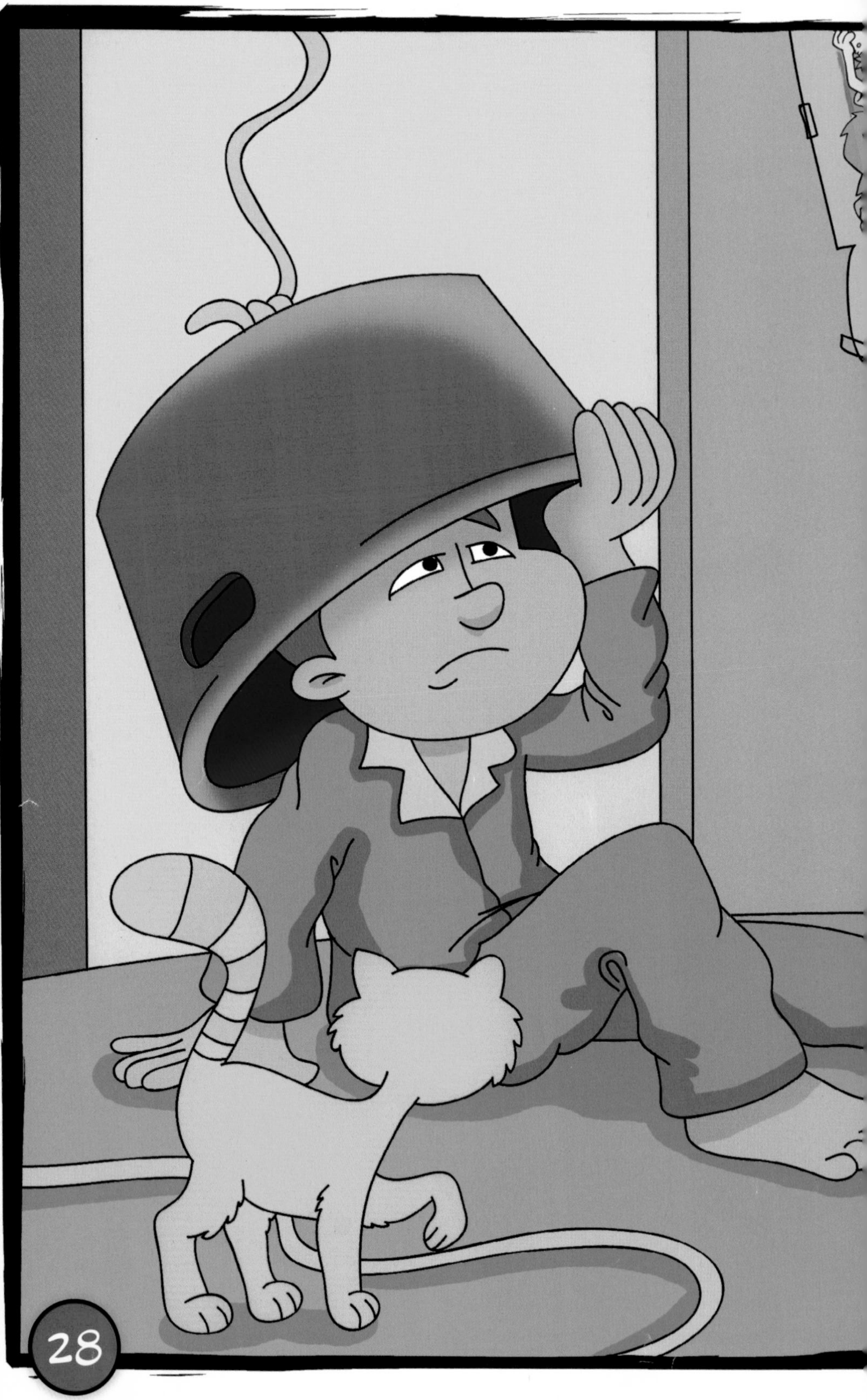

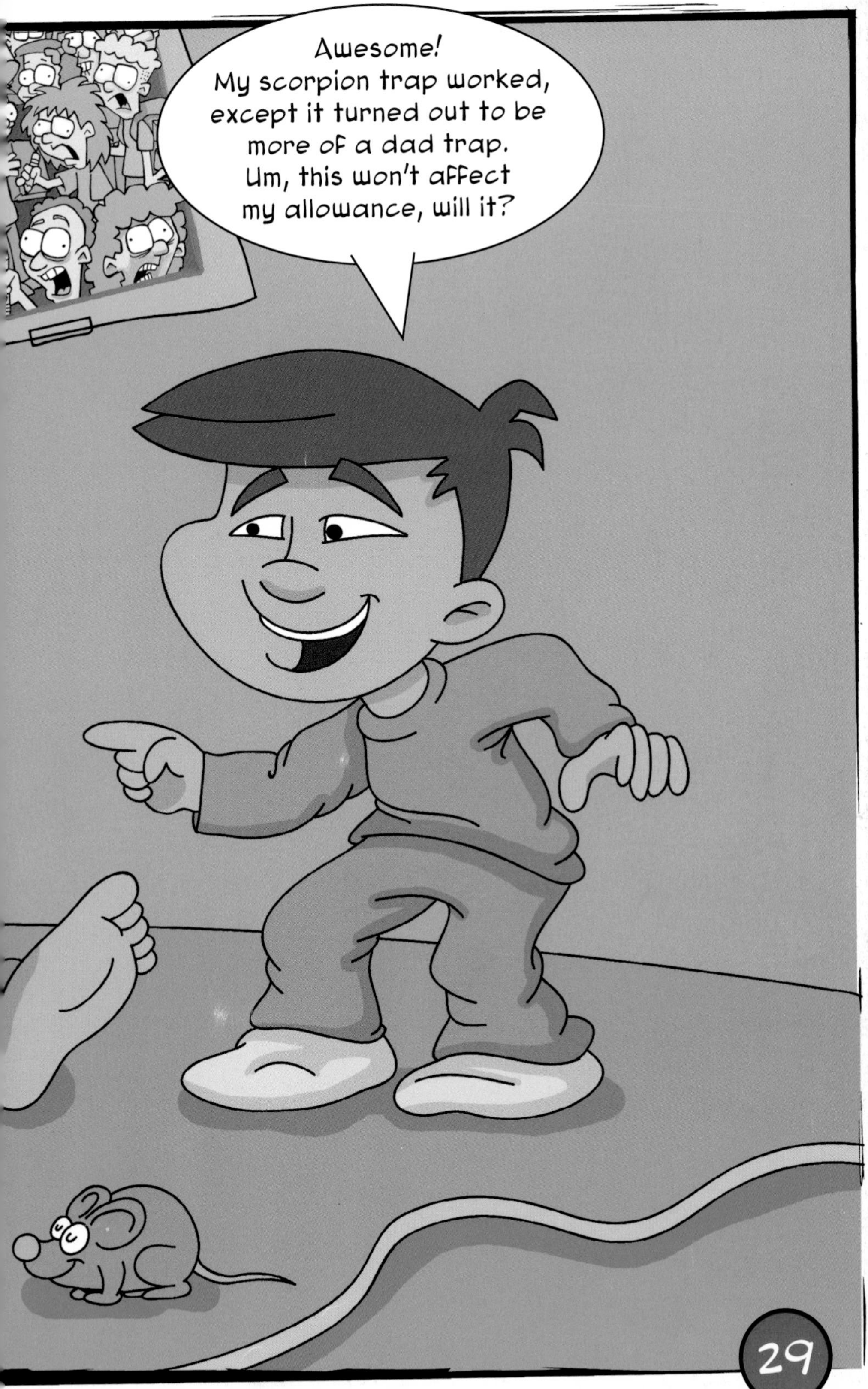
Awesome! My scorpion trap worked, except it turned out to be more of a dad trap. Um, this won't affect my allowance, will it?

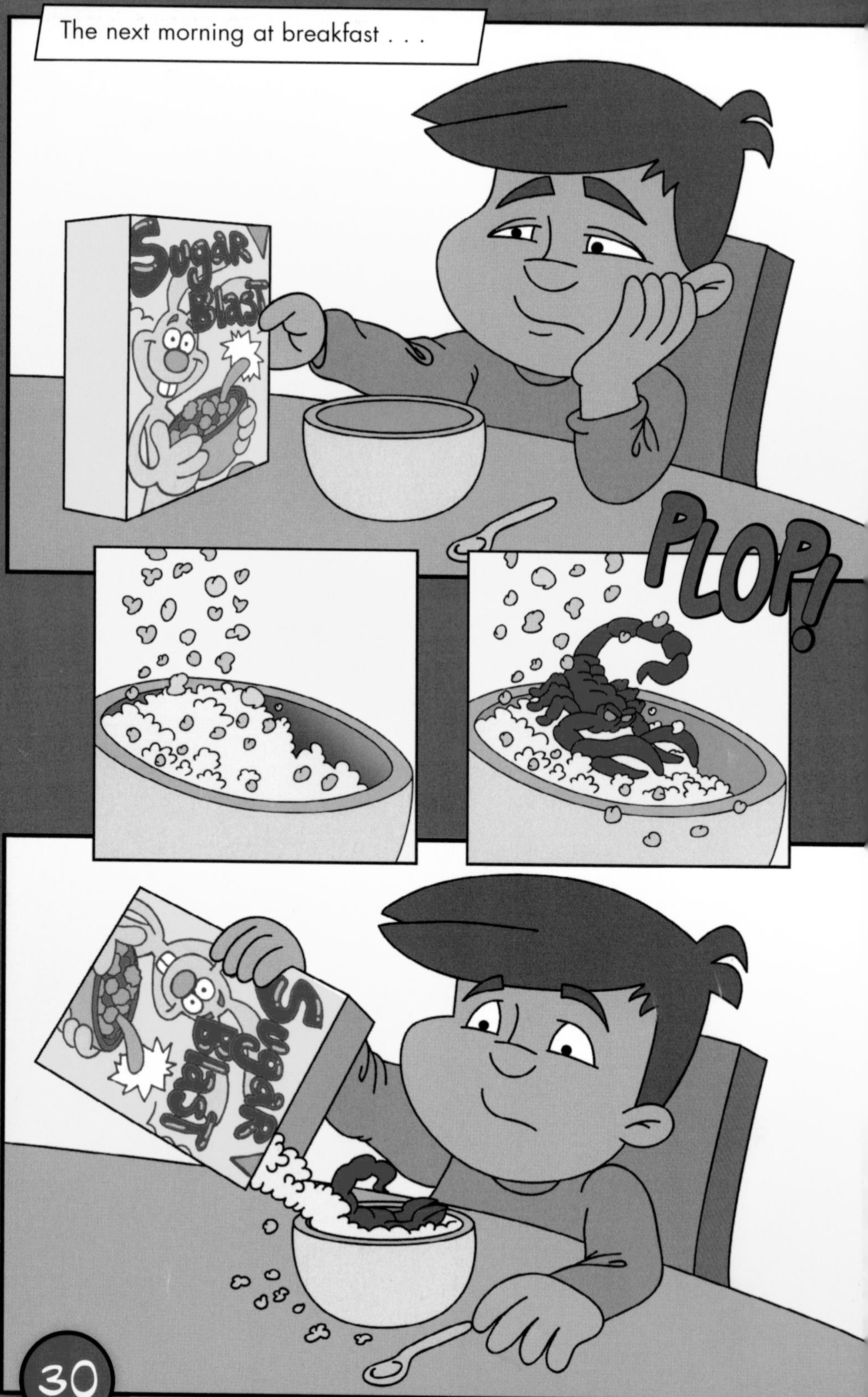

The next morning at breakfast . . .
Sugar Blast
PLOP!
Sugar Blast

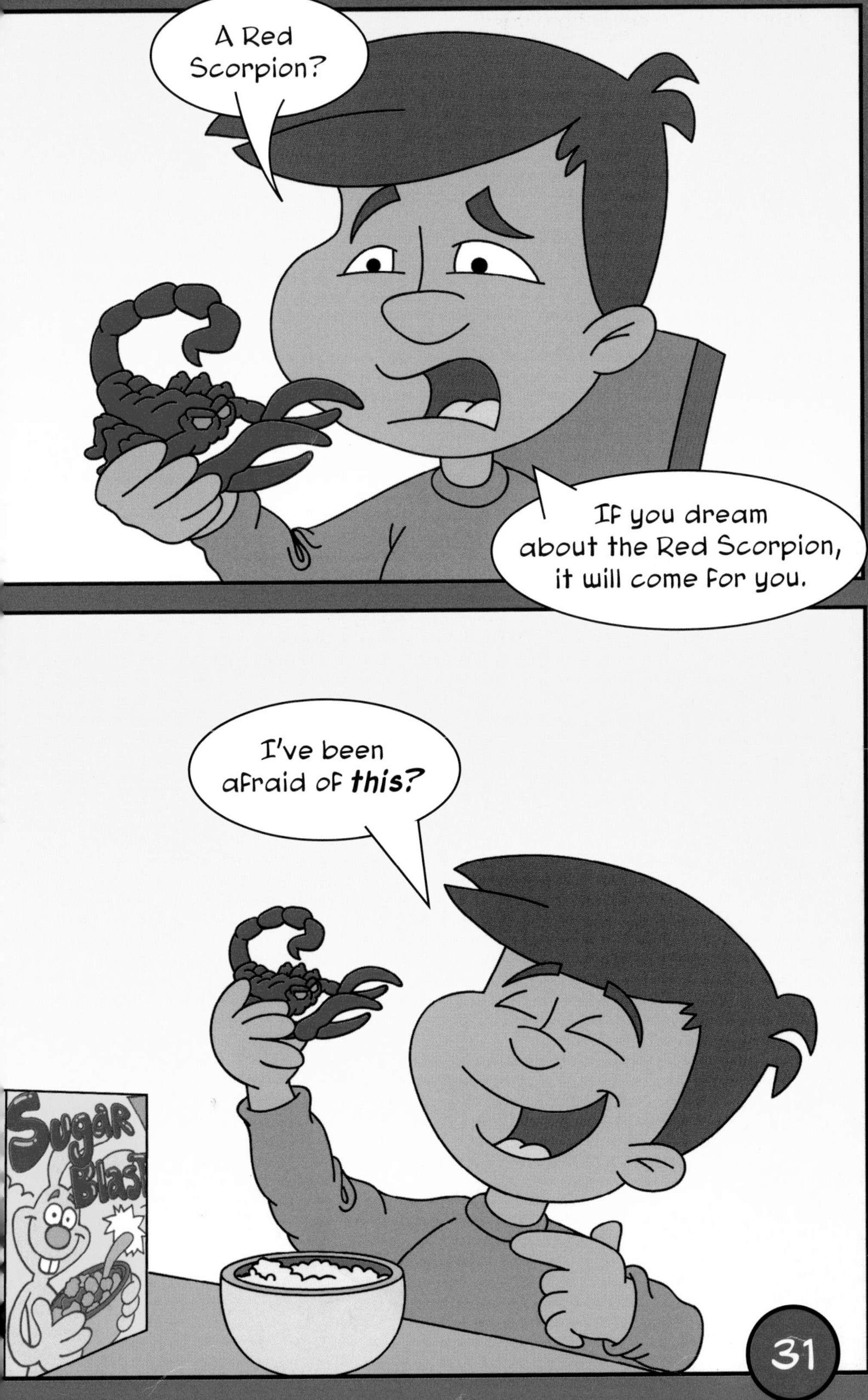
A Red Scorpion?
If you dream about the Red Scorpion, it will come for you.
I've been afraid of **this?**

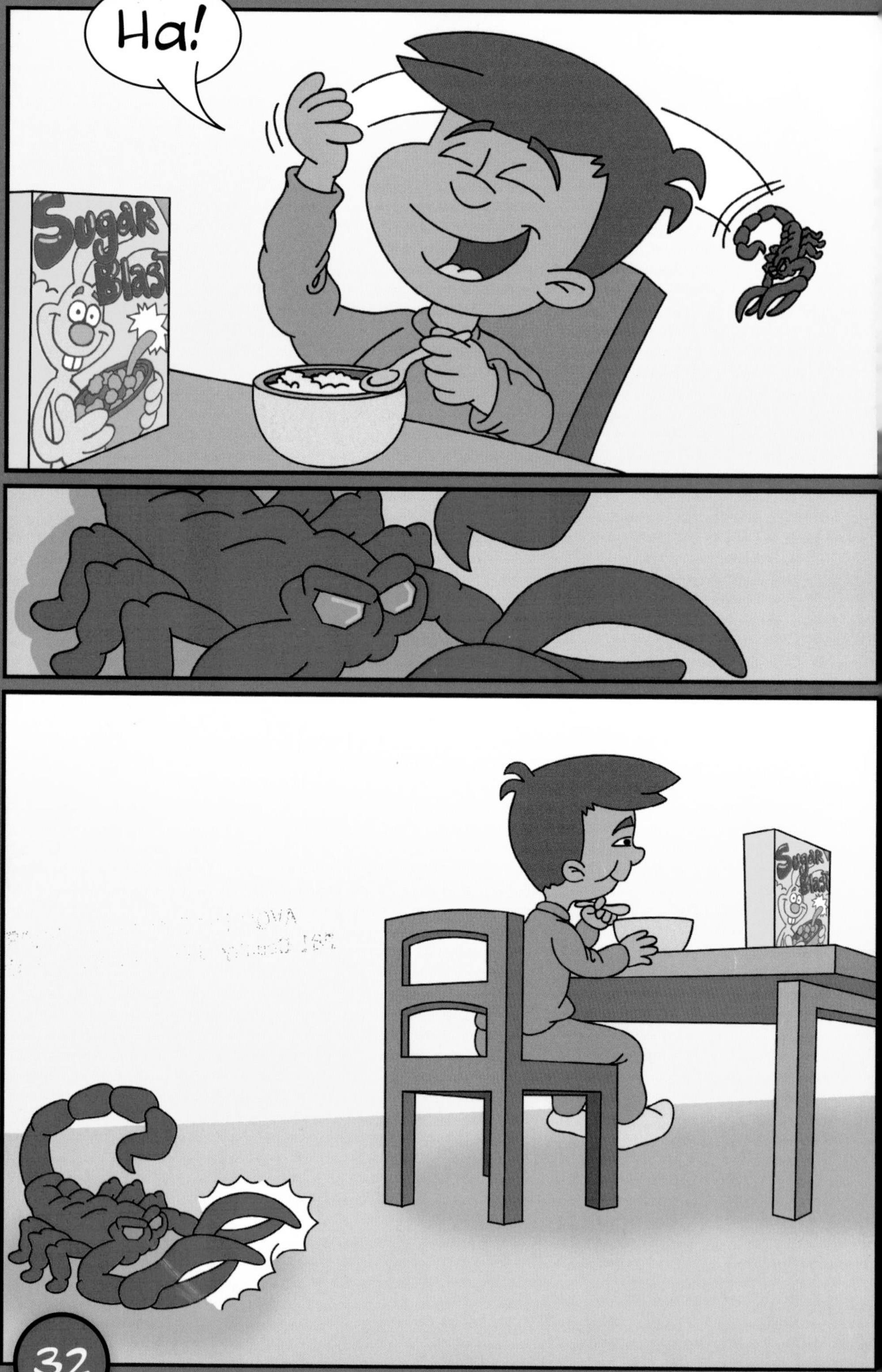
Ha!
Sugar Blast

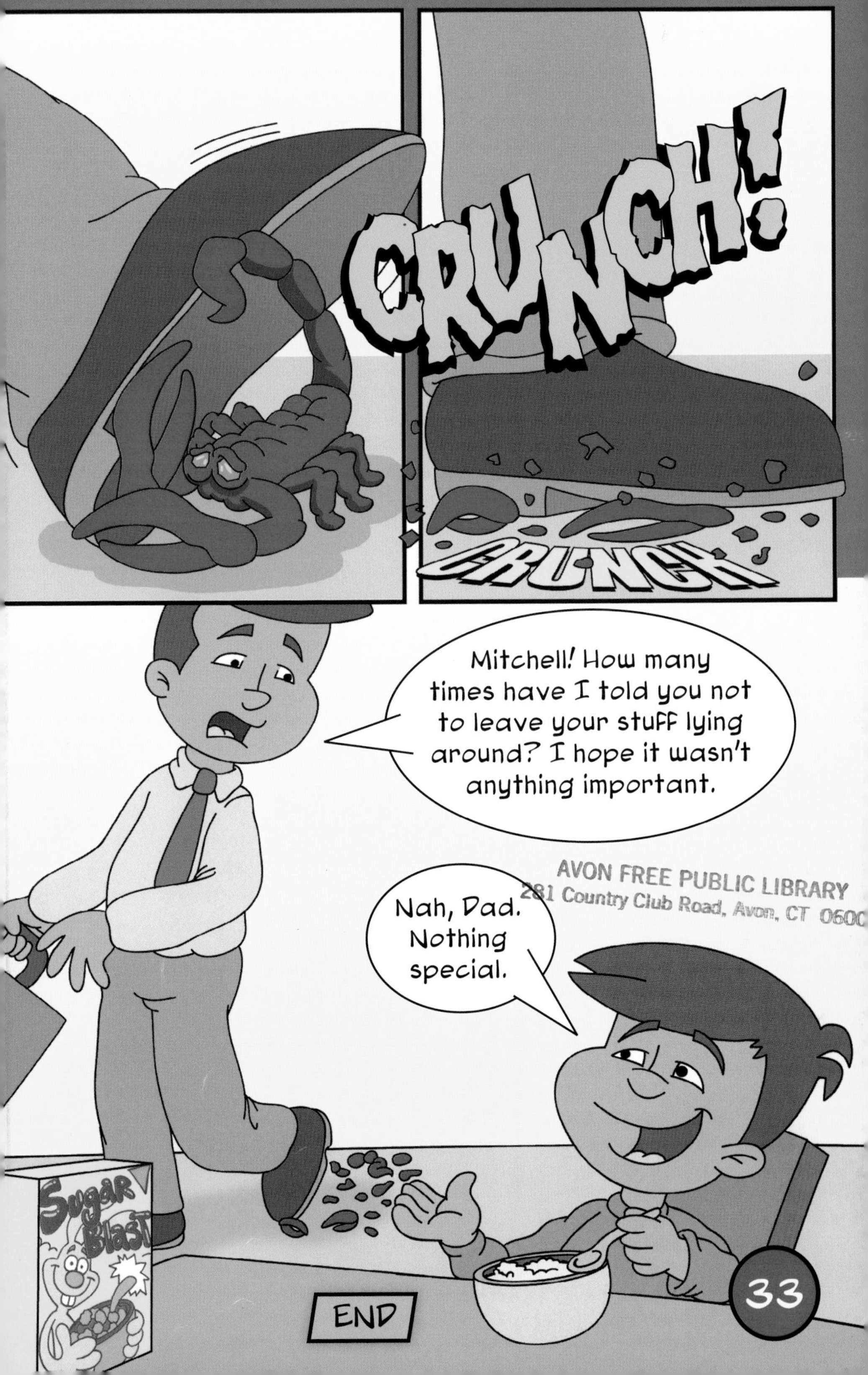
CRUNCH!
CRUNCH
Mitchell! How many times have I told you not to leave your stuff lying around? I hope it wasn't anything important.
Nah, Dad. Nothing special.
Sugar Blast
END

ABOUT THE AUTHOR

Scott Nickel has written children's books, short fiction for *Boys' Life Magazine*, humorous greeting cards, and lots of really funny knock-knock jokes. Scott is also the author of many Garfield books.

Currently, Scott lives in Indiana with his wife, two sons, four cats, a parakeet, and several sea monkeys.

ABOUT THE ILLUSTRATOR

Steve Harpster has loved to draw funny cartoons, mean monsters, and goofy gadgets since he was able to pick up a pencil. In first grade, he was able to avoid his writing assignments by working on the pictures for stories instead.

Steve was able to land a job drawing funny pictures for books, and that's really what he's best at. Steve lives in Columbus, Ohio, with his wonderful wife, Karen, and their sheepdog, Doodle.

GLOSSARY

curse (KURSS) a spell intended to harm someone, so having a younger sister or brother really isn't a curse even though it may seem like one

legend (LEJ-uhnd) a story that has been around for a long time; legends may or may not be true.

Manzitopia (man-zuh-TOH-pee-uh) a make-believe place where the Red Scorpion used to live

rock man (ROK MAN) any guy weird enough to love rocks

specimen (SPESS-uh-muhn) a sample of a larger group of things; a zoo might have specimens of deadly creatures for people to see and study safely.

Super Soak Water Blaster (SOO-pur SOHK WAW-tur BLAST-ur) the ultimate weapon for fighting off nighttime intruders

Some of these word specimens are hundreds of years old!

STINGING SCORPION SMARTS

Scorpions can have as many as 12 eyes.

The most common pet scorpion is the Emperor Scorpion. Its sting is like that of a wasp or bee. It can grow to a length of 6 inches.

Scorpions are nocturnal. This means they only move around at night, but not in people's dreams.

There are over 1500 species of scorpions, but only about 20-25 of them are dangerous to people.

Scorpions have been around for 400 million years.

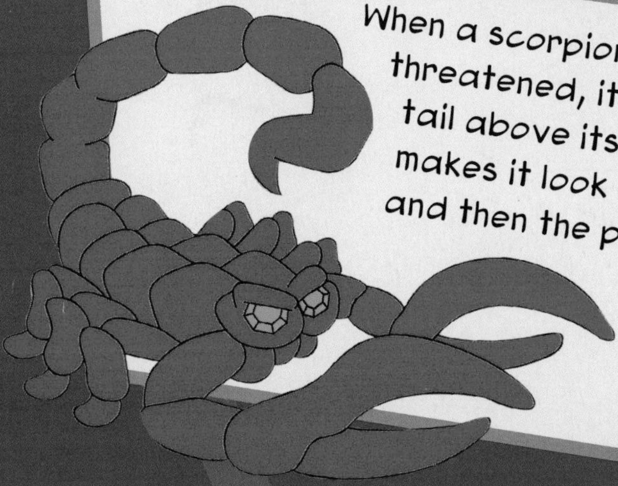

When a scorpion is threatened, it will lift its tail above its head. This makes it look even scarier, and then the predator will usually leave it alone.

DISCUSSION QUESTIONS

1.) Mitchell keeps seeing the dreaded Red Scorpion in his room. But every time he turns on the lights, it turns out to be something else. Have you ever thought you saw something in your room that wasn't really there?

2.) What would you do if you were Mitchell and you kept dreaming about the Red Scorpion?

3.) The museum guide knows a lot about amazing rocks and minerals, such as the ruby eyes of the Red Scorpion. Do you think he knows more about the scorpion than he tells the kids? Do you think he has had his own strange encounter with the creature? Why or why not?

WRITING PROMPTS

1.) Mitchell creates an amazing trap to catch the scorpion. Think about the different objects in your own room and build a trap with them. Describe your trap in detail and don't forget to tell us what you're going to catch.

2.) Oh no, you just went to the Museum of Natural History! While you were there you saw something you will never forget. Was it a dinosaur? Was it a mummy? Describe what you saw and why it scared you.

3.) We've all had bad dreams before. Write about your scariest dream and how you got over it.

INTERNET

Do you want to know more about subjects related to this book? Or are you interested in learning about other topics? Then check out FactHound, a fun, easy way to find Internet sites.

Our investigative staff has already sniffed out great sites for you!

Here's how to use FactHound:

1.) Visit www.facthound.com

2.) Select your grade level.

3.) To learn more about subjects related
to this book, type in the book's ISBN number:
1598890344. If you're looking for information
on another subject, simply type
in a keyword.

4.) Click the *Fetch It* button.

FactHound will fetch the best Internet sites for you.

www.FACTHOUND.com
SM